MW00581759

MISMET SOULS

MARISSA ADAMS

Copyright ©2022 by Marissa Adams

All rights reserved.

No part of this book may be reproduced, distributed, or transmitted in any form without written permission from the publisher or author, except as permitted by copyright law.

This book is dedicated to all of my amazing and supportive friends and family who helped me along the way to make this dream a reality.

CHAPTER ONE

MIA ARDENT SAT ON her bed, with her laptop precariously placed on her knees as she typed away, creating a fantastical world where she could be the hero of the story. She found it hard to concentrate as the late August heat found its way into her dorm room. Despite having both windows open and a fan blowing in her direction, she was still having a difficult time staying cool.

College was the point in your life where everything changed. You were supposed to find out who you really were and what you really wanted out of life. At least, that was what they always told you. Mia, in her third year at Elk Grove University, was still struggling to find herself.

She leaned back in her bed and groaned, wiping the sweat off her forehead and grabbing a hair tie from her bedside table. She pulled her long, wavy dark blue hair into a messy bun on top of her head before continuing to type, hoping to get away for as long as possible before her roommate, Thea, returned from class.

Lost in her made-up world, she jumped as Thea burst open the door to the room, music blaring from her headphones. She was jamming out with not a single care in the world, bobbing her head back and forth so that her strawberry blonde ponytail was bouncing all over the place.

Mia let out a small chuckle, watching as Thea danced around like a lunatic. Leave it to Thea to make such an entrance. She wondered how her glasses could stay on her face with all the head-banging she was doing.

The song finally ended, and Thea took off her headphones, looking in Mia's direction.

"What, is it too hot for you outside?" she said as she caught her breath, nodding toward Mia.

"Uh, yeah, it's boiling in here! You're telling me you're not dying of heat?"

"Not really." Thea shrugged as she unpacked her drawing pencils from her bag and placed them on her desk. "But then again, I've never really had a problem with the heat before."

"Lucky you," Mia said sarcastically, turning back to her laptop and reading over what she had written.

"So, what are you working on over there?" Thea said as she walked over and hopped onto her unmade bed, pushing her discarded pajamas from that morning onto the floor. "It can't be homework. It's only the first week of classes."

"Of course this isn't homework. It's a story I'm working on."

"Ah, yes, another story you won't let anyone read," she commented as she took out her phone.

"Oh, shut up," Mia joked. "You know I don't like people reading my work, not even my parents." Mia waved off her comment as Thea rolled her eyes. "And anyway, I don't work well under time constraints, so you know I don't like procrastinating until the last minute like you do."

"Wow, I'm hurt." Thea placed her hand on her heart, feigning offense for a moment. Mia just smiled and shook her head at her. "Go on."

"Getting your homework done on Friday lets you enjoy the weekend without having to worry about all that work you will inevitably have to do on Sunday night. So I just get to relax instead," she explained.

Thea thought about that for a moment. "Hm, you've got a point, I guess. Though I do have a talent for making masterpieces under a time constraint."

"I wouldn't really call that a talent," Mia said, chuckling.

Thea threw a pillow at her in response and started laughing. "Well, that's what I'm calling it!"

Mia threw the pillow back at her, and they laughed for a while before Thea got up to organize the art supplies on her desk. Mia turned back to her laptop and tried to remember where she was in her story.

It did not take long before her train of thought was interrupted again by Thea. "So, Mia, what do you think we should do to celebrate finishing this exceptional first week of our junior year?"

"What do you mean?" Mia said, looking away from the computer screen and toward Thea.

"We've gotta go celebrate! We've done something fun the past two years to finish the week off and bring those good vibes for the semester, so now we gotta make it three for three!"

"Yeah ... If I recall correctly, last year we got some rank Chinese food, and I ended up puking most of the night."

"Well ... I guess that means it'll be easy to top last year then!"

"Where do you get this never-ending source of positivity?"

"Not a clue!" she said as she made her way back over to her bed and hopped up. "Anyway, I heard there's a party over at the Alpha Beta frat house tonight, and we should definitely check it out!"

"Ew, pass. You know parties aren't my scene, especially not frat boy parties." Mia rolled her eyes and turned back to her computer. "And what kind of name is Alpha Beta, anyway? Sounds like someone just got really lazy when he wanted to make a fraternity and chose the only two Greek letters he knew."

Thea groaned and hopped off her bed. "Never mind the name, Mia," she whined, walking over to Mia and shaking her arm.

"Please reconsider going!"

Mia looked away from her, refusing to give in. "I'd really rather not."

"Please!" She continued begging. "We can just dance? I know you like dancing! Or, hey, we could make fun of the drunk people— you love doing that! Please, let's just go. It'll be so much fun! Please, please, please, plea—"

Mia put her hand over Thea's mouth. "If I say yes, will it make you shut up?"

She nodded enthusiastically in response.

"Then fine, I'll go."

"Yes! I promise you won't regret it! And hey, maybe you'll even meet someone there." She raised her eyebrows suggestively.

"You know I don't really care about being in a relationship right now, Thea."

"I know, but that doesn't mean I can't still dream of my best friend finding some happiness with another human being! That'll certainly give you something to write about, whatever it is you write about anyway ..." she said as she tried to sneak a peek at Mia's laptop.

Mia quickly grabbed it from her and held it against her chest. "No peeking!"

She huffed and walked over to her closet. "Fine, but I will see what you're writing someday!" She started rummaging through her clothes, looking for something to wear for the night.

Pulling out a flirty floral print dress and holding it in front of her, Thea twirled in front of the mirror. She wrinkled her nose as she gave it one more look before tossing it to the side.

Mia could not understand why it was so important for her to find the perfect outfit for this party. It was not like it was anything special.

"Hm." Thea stared at herself in the mirror, mulling over what was in her closet. She snapped her fingers as she came up with an idea. "I know just the thing!"

She pulled out a black high-necked crop top that zipped up the front and a pair of ripped, black skinny jeans.

When she finished picking out something for herself, she went over to Mia's closet and started looking through it. Mia shut down her laptop and hopped off her bed. "Hey, what're you—"

"If we're going to a party, you're going to need to wear something other than that 'comfy nerd' look you've got going on."

Mia looked down at her comic book print tank top and black leggings, not understanding what was wrong with her outfit.

"I happen to like the 'comfy nerd' look." She said defiantly, crossing her arms.

"And you rock it, but not for a frat party." She said, handing Mia a black tank top with lace accents and a pair of jean shorts.

Mia groaned at her and reluctantly grabbed the outfit, already regretting saying yes to her. She brought it over to her bed and changed. When she finished, she turned around to see Thea had taken down her strawberry blonde hair, letting it fall loosely down to the middle of her back.

The crop top and skinny jeans she chose flattered her tall frame perfectly. It was a shocking change from her usually sporty look of ponytails, leggings, and sneakers. It made Mia feel self-conscious.

She walked over to her closet and looked at herself in the mirror as Thea put in contacts and fixed her makeup. She wasn't exactly overweight, but standing next to Thea in her skin-tight outfit, she couldn't help but think about how she could never pull off something like that.

"There you go, girl, looking ready to par-tay!" Thea said, dancing towards Mia and grabbing her hand. She twirled her in a circle and then looked her up and down again. "Are you gonna do anything with your hair, or is the messy bun a look you just can't ditch?" she said, reaching for Mia's hair.

"You already made me change. Don't push it with the hair too." Mia said, backing away from her.

Thea frowned at her. "And no chance at a little makeup then?"

"Absolutely not." Mia crossed her arms defiantly.

"Not even just a teensy bit of eyeliner?"

"No."

"Mascara?"

"Thea!"

"All right, all right, miss cranky pants, let's go then!"

"You shouldn't be calling me names when you're the one making me go out tonight."

"Yeah, yeah, whatever. Come on, let's get going!"

Thea grabbed Mia's hand and pulled her towards the door.

CHAPTER TWO

THE PARTY WAS THE usual kind, with lots of underage drinking and dancing. The house itself was large and on the older side, with rich mahogany walls and two stories full of people partying the night away. Thea was enjoying herself, swaying her hips on the makeshift dance floor in the living room, talking to some skinny black-haired boy with a faux hawk, and Mia could swear she saw her take a shot or two. She'd be twenty-one in a few months, so she didn't really care, but that didn't stop her from keeping a watchful eye on Thea.

She only took her eyes off her to look at her phone and send a quick text. Erika, one of her friends from back home, was texting her about her lousy first week of school. She'd be happy to hear Mia was actually out at a party, no matter how lame she thought it was.

"So, which one's yours?" a voice said from next to her, drawing Mia out of her own thoughts. Looking to her right, she saw a tall boy with curly red hair looking at her. His face was hard and angular, with freckles covering almost every inch. He seemed to be nothing but muscle, and by the look of his letterman jacket, he belonged to the fraternity that was throwing this party. By Thea's standards he might have been attractive, but looking at him, Mia couldn't help but smell the beer on his breath and feel disgusted. He took a swig out of his red solo cup as he waited for her to respond.

"Excuse me?" Mia said, not sure what he meant.

"You've been watching the dance floor for a really long time. That means you're doing one of three things." He started counting on his fingers. "You're longing to be out there dancing yourself, you're people watching, or you're looking out for someone. I went with the last one as a guess because of that serious look on your face."

"You've been watching me?" She chuckled nervously and shifted her weight. "'Cause that's not creepy or anything." She turned her eyes back towards Thea, hoping this stranger would just go away.

"Wow, that's cold," he said, not taking the hint. He took another swig from his cup before introducing himself. "I'm Jared, by the way. Was I right in assuming you're looking out for someone over there?"

Mia sighed, obviously annoyed. "Yes, I am. What are you, some kind of psych major or something?"

He laughed at that. "Minor actually. How'd you guess?"

"You've got good observational skills, but you ask too many questions. Not super hard to figure out." She said coldly, continuing to avoid looking at this boy.

"So then, what do you major in?" He took yet another sip from the cup. Mia hoped he wasn't drinking anything too strong; otherwise, this would get annoying really fast.

"I don't see why that matters to a stranger." She said, crossing her arms and standing up straighter to seem more confident than she actually felt.

"Hey, I'm just trying to make small talk here, and y'know, technically, we're not strangers. I told you my name, after all, though you never mentioned yours."

"Probably because I don't like to give my name to people I just meet, especially not drunk guys at a house party." She judgingly looked him up and down, thinking that being blunt might finally get him to leave. "And I'm not much for small talk, anyway. I'm just here because my friend wanted me to come along with her." She turned away from him again and pulled out her phone to see if Erika had texted her back.

"Wow, that was… a lot." He laughed and took another sip from his cup. "So…" he started, ignoring her cue for him to leave her alone once again. "You must be pretty good friends with this girl if she convinced you to come to a party you so blatantly don't wanna be at."

Mia rolled her eyes and shoved her phone back into her pocket before responding to him. "We've been roommates for two years now, so yeah, I'd say we're pretty close." She looked back over at Thea and saw she was dancing close with the black-haired boy she had been talking to for the past hour. Mia made a face, not trusting a stranger to be that close to her best friend. Jared seemed to notice the change in her demeanor.

"Hey, maybe you should get a drink or something, loosen up a bit, y'know?"

"Sorry, I don't drink. And I don't need to 'loosen up.' I just need to make sure my roommate doesn't end up in any sort of trouble."

"Oh, come on, I'm sure she'll be fine. Just come get a drink with me real quick. We'll be there and back before she even notices."

Mia looked at the cup in his hand and then back at him. "You already have a drink, and I really don't think you need another one. Besides, like I already told you, I don't drink."

"Fine, no drinking for you then, but that doesn't mean we can't have a little fun." He grabbed Mia's waist and tried to pull her close.

"Hey! What are you doing? Get away from me!" she yelled as she pushed him away. He spilled the small amount of alcohol that was left in his cup onto his shirt as he stumbled backwards.

He wasn't expecting Mia to push him away, and he looked at

her like she was a challenge to be won. He tossed his cup to the ground and stalked back over to her.

"Playing hard to get, huh? Well, I'm always up for a little challenge." He said as he got close to Mia again.

Forcefully, he grabbed her arm and pulled her back towards him. Swinging her around, he pushed her between himself and the wall.

"Hey! Stop! What're you—" He slammed his lips against hers and attempted to make out with her. She struggled against him while he shoved her harder against the wall, pushing his tongue into her mouth.

"Get off of me!" she said, shoving her knee into his stomach and then pushing him away as hard as she could. He groaned and stumbled backwards a couple of steps.

"C'mon now, don't be like that. I thought we were hitting it off," he said, chuckling as he walked back towards her one last time.

"Don't take another step towards me!" she shouted at him as loud as she could. He stopped, surprised, as a couple of other party goers stared in their direction.

"C'mon, don't be such a tease. You clearly want me."

"No. I don't. Now leave me alone!" she yelled, stalking past him and straight for Thea.

"What a bitch," he mumbled just loud enough for her to hear as he walked back over to his friends. He immediately began talking to them and they all started laughing, presumably at what had just happened.

"We need to go," Mia said as she walked up to Thea, grabbing her hand, and pulled her away from her mystery boy.

He looked upset by her intrusion but not surprised.

"What? Why? Did something happen? Why do you look so upset?" She blurted out one question after another as Mia dragged her to the exit, leaving the boy she was talking to standing there.

He ruffled his faux hawk in confusion before walking away from the dance floor and towards Jared and his friends.

"I'm fine. I just don't wanna be here anymore."

"Mia. I can tell when you're lying. Now just tell me what's going on."

"I will. Just… not here, okay?"

"Okay," she said kindly. "We'll leave. I've celebrated enough, anyway. Why don't we do something you wanna do when we get back?"

Mia nodded as they left the property and headed back to their dorm.

"My god, Mia, I'm so sorry. You were totally right—we should've stayed home tonight!" Thea gasped after hearing what happened.

They had stopped walking near the edge of campus, the full moon casting a dim glow over them.

"No, don't say that!" Mia groaned. "You were having a lot of fun dancing, and I was fine until that asshole showed up." She rubbed her arm awkwardly and shrugged. "I'm sure I'll forget about it soon anyway, and I should've just walked away when I saw he was drinking. So don't blame yourself."

"Don't you dare go blaming yourself for this either, Mia!" Thea yelled, walking closer to her and grabbing her hands. "He sexually assaulted you. It's HIS fault. No one else's. And he's lucky we're not gonna press charges against him for it." She paused for a moment and a crazy look came into her eyes. She dropped Mia's hands and put her own to her chin, thinking. "Or maybe we should press charges. That'll teach him for ever messing with my best friend!"

Mia just stared at her.

"Are you being serious right now?"

"Mia, when am I ever not serious?" She gave her the fakest serious look she could.

"Almost every other time I talk to you?" Mia responded

sarcastically. Thea just shrugged and gave her a big smile. "Anyway, I don't really wanna think about it anymore, so let's just forget it, okay?" Mia tried her best to give a smile, but it appeared pained. "Besides, you looked like you were getting friendly with that guy tonight." She bumped her elbow lightly against Thea's arm, trying to lighten the mood and change the subject.

Thea giggled a bit. "Yeah, he was fun, real quiet and mysterious, though. I basically did all the talking. Not really my type, so I doubt I'll be seeing him again."

"Quiet type? Are you sure you weren't just talking so much that he couldn't get a word in?" Mia joked.

"Hey!" Thea playfully hit Mia on the arm. "I do not talk that much!"

"As someone who lives with you, I beg to differ!"

"Well, someone has to fill in the silence since you don't like to talk a lot. Unless you count sarcastic commentary."

"You got me there." Mia shrugged.

They walked again as Thea hummed to herself, leaving Mia with only her thoughts weighing on her mind like a plague.

They meandered their way down the sidewalk as the town melted away into the campus. The large forest that surrounded the buildings felt like it was closing around them the closer they got to the dorms. The crickets were louder in this part of the campus, but even their chirping mixed with Thea's humming did nothing to stop her mind from replaying the scene with Jared repeatedly.

She never wanted to feel that helpless again.

Out of nowhere, the crickets stopped their chirping, leaving an eerie silence hanging over them. Both Mia and Thea froze, looking towards the woods on their left, as a grim feeling settled in.

What could be so dangerous that the crickets would be so silent?

"Mia?" Thea said hesitantly.

"Shh!" Mia hushed her.

Whatever it was could be dangerous, and sound could drive

it to them.

Then she saw it, the blur of something big and furry. Her eyes went wide, and she shoved Thea.

"Run, Thea!" she hissed at her as they sprinted back to the dorm.

Once they were standing in front of the building, they stopped to catch their breath.

"Wh-what… what was that?" Thea asked between breaths.

"I… I don't know. It… looked like some kind of… giant animal," Mia said, almost gasping for air.

Thea stood up straight and placed her hands on her hips.

"An animal? What, like… a bear?"

"Yeah, maybe…" Mia scrunched her eyes closed and rubbed her temples, trying to remember what she saw. "It was long, though, and fast."

"Like a wolf then?" Thea said enthusiastically.

"It was way too big to be a wolf," Mia said, crossing her arms and shifting her weight nervously.

"Maybe it was a werewolf!" Thea laughed.

"Yeah, right!" Mia said.

"Hey, you never know. It is a full moon!"

She chuckled a bit. "Well, whatever it was, let's hope we don't run into it again."

"Definitely!" Thea turned to walk into their dorm. "So, what do you wanna do now? We could watch a movie or—"

Mia stopped listening as her best friend walked inside. She looked back out towards the woods again. Just what was that thing they saw?

CHAPTER THREE

A CELL PHONE RINGING AWOKE Elliott in the early morning. Oh, how he absolutely hated being woken up after a full moon. It felt like he had just crawled into his bed mere minutes ago. He groaned and rolled over. Brushing his dark, messy hair out of his face, he patted around his nightstand until he found his phone.

"Hello?" he grumbled.

"Elliott? It's me. We need to talk."

"Mom? Isn't it a little early for—"

"Elliott, this is serious. Something happened last night." She sounded frantic.

Elliott sat up, his senses suddenly on high alert. "What is it? What happened?"

A million scenarios flew through his head before his mom even answered. Was his brother hurt somehow? Or maybe someone saw them and their secret was out?

"It's—it's Ava," his mother stuttered.

Elliott's heart dropped. His sister-in-law. His brother's

soulmate.

"She's in the hospital. They're saying that it was a car accident, but—but we're not so sure. We think your father might have had something to do with it."

His father? He knew his father hated the very idea of mates because he wanted to keep their werewolf bloodline "pure," but he never thought he would stoop to attacking them just so he could marry off his brother to a pureblood. His backwards way of thinking was the whole reason Elliott left Elk Grove.

"If she's in the hospital, that means she's going to be okay, though… right? She's recovering?"

"She's got a lot of broken bones, and she was badly burned. She was lucky that someone found the car and pulled her out before it completely went up in flames, but it still isn't looking good." She paused, giving Elliott some time to process what she had told him. He could feel the dread slowly setting in at the possibility of losing his sister-in-law.

Ava was such a kind person. She accepted his brother Tristan without a second thought after he told her they were all werewolves. She didn't deserve something like this to happen to her.

He could feel his breath getting shaky and was struggling to keep the phone in his hands.

"Honey… you've got to come back home. Your brother is going to need your support."

"Mom… I can't just pack up and leave. School starts up again next month, and Zeke and I have another couple months on this lease."

"We'll figure it out. We just need you home."

It had been a little over a month since that day, and since then, Ava had passed. Her funeral was tragic, and Elliott had never seen his brother so distraught. His family's grief had convinced him to uproot the entirely new life he had made in the past three years, just to bring him back to his hometown.

He transferred schools pretty easily, though that was the least of his worries considering his stepfather was the dean. Lucky enough, an apartment was easy to come by as well. He was not, however, happy to be back in class again.

Elliott struggled to keep his eyes open as his American History professor drawled on, reading verbatim from a PowerPoint on the big screen at the front of the stuffy lecture hall. He let out a long yawn as he pushed his dark brown hair out of his eyes.

He was still recovering from the full moon that past Friday. Between moving and classes, followed by a forced transformation, he was absolutely beat. He was actually a little jealous that Zeke had gotten to go out and party the weekend away while he was stuck as a wolf for one night and then struggling to sleep for the following two.

He had gotten too close to the campus during the full moon, drawn by the scent of something there. He almost didn't realize what he was doing until he heard the scared voice of a girl calling to her friend. He hoped they didn't actually see him, but the thought of getting that close to humans without even realizing it scared him.

"And don't forget, there will be a quiz on Chapter Two at the end of the week, so make sure you all log on to the online portal and get that done." The voice of his professor ending the class drew him out of his racing thoughts. "Class dismissed," he said, shutting off the PowerPoint and gathering his things.

"Ugh, finally." Elliott groaned, pulling himself out of his seat and shoving his notebook into his bag. He stretched out his arms and back as several joints popped at the movement. He let out a relieved sigh. Sitting like that for so long always made him feel stir crazy, and the seats were just a little too small for him.

He made his way out of the lecture hall and immediately

felt a throbbing in his head. He stopped walking and rubbed his temples. When the pain didn't go away, he frowned. He rarely ever got headaches. This was highly unusual. Chalking it up to the lack of sleep, he continued on his way down the staircase, wanting to get home as quickly as possible.

As he made it to the first floor, he laid eyes on a short girl walking through the front doors. Her wavy dark blue hair was pulled into two low pigtails, with just the tiniest bit of fringe framing her round face perfectly. He couldn't help but stare at her. She was beautiful, and the quirky heart shape of her glasses made him smile for a reason he couldn't understand. He felt his face flush, thinking about a stranger this way; he hadn't had a crush since high school, so why would just seeing her make him feel like this?

A group of boys who were gossiping stopped and watched her as she walked by. A redhead with a large bruise on the side of his face looked at her like she was his prey. Elliott vaguely remembered Zeke telling him he had beaten someone up last Friday for coming on to some girl who clearly didn't want it. He wondered if this was that boy.

Elliott felt rage bubbling to the surface at the way this boy stared at her.

"Well, would you look who it is? The little tease from Friday night's party," the red-headed boy commented as she passed by, keeping her head down. His friends all laughed as if that was the funniest thing they'd heard all day.

Elliott ground his teeth. *What are these boys, fifteen or something? Who teases a girl like that in college?*

She stopped and spun around on them. "A tease? I don't recall ever even showing signs I was interested in doing anything with you. It's not my fault you're too dense to take a hint."

Elliot let a grin slip out. This girl had some nerve to her.

The boy's friends let out a series of "oohs" as his face lit up almost as red as his own hair.

She spun back around with a smirk on her face and attempted to walk away again, but the jerk grabbed her arm and yanked her towards him.

Elliott growled, surprising himself at the sudden urge to hurt these boys for daring to lay a hand on this girl he didn't even know. He felt a strange pull towards her, and it scared him to think about it.

She turned towards the boy and her body tensed up. Though he couldn't see her face, Elliott knew she was glaring at him.

"Come on, it's just a joke," he said, giving her a smile as if it would make everything better.

"Yeah... it wasn't really funny to me," she said, yanking her arm out of his hand.

She spun on her heels and made her way straight towards Elliott.

The look on her face was one of pure rage, and even though she didn't look it, he could tell she wasn't one to be messed with.

He watched her walk towards him and couldn't pull himself away from her intense gaze. Panicking, he attempted to move out of her way, but they ended up running right into each other.

His shoulder hit her awkwardly, and she fell backwards. With inhuman speed, Elliott caught her in his arm. The two stuck in a position that looked like the dip of a waltz.

"I'm so sorry," he said, but as soon as he made eye contact with her, it was as if the entire world enveloped them in a fog.

Her scent surrounded him, the sweet smell of cinnamon wafting through the air. It reminded him of the snickerdoodles his mother would make for him as a child when he was upset, and it was utterly intoxicating. His body completely relaxed to her touch, and he wanted to pull her close to him, to let her scent completely envelop him.

Elliott felt like he was in a trance, unable to look away from her beautiful brown eyes.

This couldn't possibly be...

"Um... excuse me?" a voice as soft as silk said, breaking through the haze in his head.

The fog that surrounded his thoughts slowly dissolved.

"Hm?" he hummed as his focus returned.

"Um, thanks for the save, but you can pull me up now," the girl said with an uncomfortable look on her face. He was still holding her in that awkward position.

Oh, man, just how long had he been holding her there? Seconds? Minutes? It felt like an eternity, but also like it hadn't been long enough.

Elliott shook his head and blinked a few times, the last remnants of the brain fog disappearing.

"Right. Sorry," he said, pulling her up and sheepishly looking away.

He could feel his face flushing in a feeling of embarrassment that he'd never felt before. People were staring, and the last thing he needed was attention to be on him. It just made him feel even more uncomfortable than he already was.

"It's, um... it's fine," she said, looking at the ground, clearly unsure of what to say after such a strange experience. "I ran into you anyway, so it's mostly my fault."

"No, it's, uh... it was my fault, really," he said, blinking a few more times and rubbing his temples to clear his head. Miraculously, his headache had completely vanished. Reality had finally caught up to him as he processed exactly what had just happened.

"Hey, are you okay?" she asked, concern lacing through her voice.

"Yeah, sorry. I've gotta go," he hastily said, pushing past her and heading straight for the exit.

He felt bad just leaving her in the dust like that... He felt bad leaving her at all, actually. This strange need to be with this girl was enveloping every sense in his body, but he knew he had to fight it. If only to protect her.

As he made his way outside the building, he pulled out

his phone and called Zeke. It rang a few times before going to voicemail.

"Damn it, Zeke!" He tried calling again. Maybe letting it ring a second time would convince him to get up and actually answer the phone.

It was mid-afternoon, but it wasn't unusual for Zeke to still be asleep. He didn't go to school, and he hadn't found a job yet, so of course he would just be sleeping the day away.

"This is Zeke. Leave a voicemail or don't. I probably won't respond, anyway." The phone chimed with a beep to leave a message.

Elliott let out an exasperated groan. "Zeke, this is the worst possible time for you to be sleeping! Listen, dude, something just happened to me and I can't really get into it over the phone. After what happened with Ava..." He paused and looked around to see if anyone was listening to him. "I just shouldn't talk about it in the open, but if you do decide to wake up at some point in the next century or so, just give me a call. I'll be at my mom's if you're looking for me."

He hung up and shoved his phone in his pocket, then sprinted as fast as he could to his car without drawing suspicion to himself.

CHAPTER FOUR

A S THE BOY LEFT Mia standing there dumbfounded at what had just happened, Thea walked through the front door of the building. He passed by her without even noticing Thea's presence, but Thea definitely noticed him.

She couldn't blame her, either. He was incredibly handsome. He was tall, with a stocky build, and his dark brown hair accentuated his bright blue eyes. Those eyes that seemed to gaze directly into her soul…

Thea turned towards Mia and immediately caught her eye from across the hall, following Mia's gaze towards the boy who had just walked out the front door. She gave Mia a wink and put her hands up in a gesture that said "nice taste."

She noticed the heat rising in her cheeks and looked away from Thea, embarrassed at the blush she knew was growing over her face. She rubbed her arm where the boy had been holding her. His touch felt strange, and he left her feeling numb and confused as soon as he let her go.

As Thea neared Jared and his gang, one boy whistled at her.

She didn't even look at them as she passed by, just flipping them off instead as she continued walking.

"What a bunch of animals," she said as she caught up to Mia.

"Ugh, tell me about it," Mia said, crossing her arms as she stared back at the front doors where her mystery boy had left. A small part of her wished he would walk back in, just so she could look at him again.

"Did he try anything? Do I need to go back there and beat him up for you?"

"I can hold my own, thank you very much. I'm a big, strong girl who can fight her own battles," she said, finally looking at Thea.

They both laughed as they started up the stairs towards their next class.

"If you say so."

"Besides, it looked like someone beat you to it already," Mia said. "Did you see the giant bruise on his face?"

"I did! I wonder how he got it…" Thea said. "Maybe someone saw what happened and was defending your honor?"

Mia laughed. "Well, whatever it was for, he probably deserved it."

They entered the lecture hall and took a seat in the back row so they could continue their gossip without disturbing anyone.

"Anyway, who was that fine piece of boy you were checking out when I walked in?" she asked, nudging Mia with her elbow.

Mia scoffed at her but was betrayed by her own body when she felt the flush appear on her cheeks again. "I wasn't checking him out. I just had the strangest interaction with him."

Mia leaned on her elbow and looked away towards the front of the classroom, thinking about what happened all over again. There was a weird feeling in the pit of her stomach. It was uncomfortable and upsetting that she couldn't pinpoint exactly what it was.

"Strange? Strange how?" Thea's voice cut through Mia's thoughts.

Mia sighed and turned back towards her.

"Well, after Jared tried to call me a tease—"

"Whoa, hold up. He called you a tease? Now I know he needs to get his ass whooped," Thea said, standing up to go back downstairs. Mia pushed her back down into her seat.

"Calm down, Thea. I told you I handled it, remember?"

Thea looked very disappointed that she wouldn't be beating anyone up today, even though Mia knew it was all talk. She'd never even seen Thea swat a fly before, always insisting on catching it and bringing it back outside.

"Anyway, I was sorta pissed after the interaction, wasn't watching where I was walking, and ended up running right into this guy."

"Oh, sounds romantic," Thea sang.

"Please hold your unnecessary commentary until the end of the story," Mia said sarcastically.

"Right, sorry." She chuckled.

"I fell, and he caught me. But then he just held me there, staring at me for, like, a full two minutes!"

"He just... held you there?"

"Yes! It was like he was frozen in place. It felt SO awkward."

Mia decided it would probably be best to leave out the strange feeling she got when she looked into his eyes, and the warmth of his touch that she could still feel on her arm. God only knew what Thea would have to say about all of that.

"That does sound really weird. He gets points off the weirdness scale, though 'cause he is really hot."

"Thea! Not the point!" she said, smacking her on the arm.

"What is the point, then? So you had a weird interaction with a guy. This shit happens. It's college, after all."

"Yeah, I don't think that's a reasonable explanation at all. The point is... I don't really know? I've got bad luck this year or something. It didn't start out great with the whole Jared thing, and now it's going downhill real fast."

"Don't count your year over just yet. There's still a chance to make it the best one ever!"

"Seriously, where can I get your unlimited supply of optimism from?" Mia said, leaning back in her chair and crossing her arms.

Thea laughed. "I don't know. It's just a feeling I have."

"Well, if I've learned anything about your 'feelings,' it's that they should be taken with a grain of salt."

The professor finally walked in, her heels clacking at the front of the lecture hall. The class quieted as she pulled up her lecture on the screen and began her lesson.

"Well, that's my cue," Thea said, pulling out her sketchbook as the professor spoke quickly.

"I don't know how you absorb information by just drawing and not taking notes, but it's so not fair," Mia said as she scrawled the information her professor spat out in her notebook.

Thea shrugged. "I don't know either, but it sure is a useful talent!"

Mia rolled her eyes and smiled at Thea, who was now thoroughly involved in whatever art piece she was working on this week.

Mia tried her best to keep up with the professor and her note-keeping, but her mind kept wandering back to that boy from the hallway. Who was he, and what had him so entranced as he held her there? And why did her heart flutter a bit when she thought about how pretty his blue eyes were to look at?

CHAPTER FIVE

ELLIOTT ROUNDED THE CORNER into the cul-de-sac, his mother's large white house coming into view. It was an older styled home, but she fixed it up with his stepfather so it shone like new. The wrap-around porch with the swing was where he often spent his nights in high school, if he wasn't out running through the forest behind the house, just dreaming of the day when he'd get out of this dreary little town and away from his father. Yet, here he was once again, back to his old life of looking over his shoulder to make sure his father wasn't lurking around, and even worse? He now had a soulmate, a very human soulmate, that his father would definitely try to get rid of.

He sighed, thinking about how his life ended up like this as he pulled into his mother's driveway.

His younger half sister, Lucy, was walking out the front door. She saw his car and rushed over, her light brown pigtails bobbing up and down as she made her way toward him. He rolled down his window as the car came to a stop.

She leaned in towards the car. "You're really gonna pull in here just as I'm leaving? I haven't seen you in months!"

Her cherry blossom scented perfume assaulted his nose as she leaned on the window, and he had to stifle a cough before responding to her.

"Sorry, Lu, I just gotta talk to Mom about something. Where are you headed off to, anyway?"

"The mall. I've gotta get something to wear for homecoming. It is my last one, after all."

Of course she was headed to the mall. That explained the large amount of perfume and the flirty floral print dress. She was probably going there to find a date, just as much as she was there to find a nice dress. It made him shiver to think how old his baby sister was getting.

"Yeah, well, you won't miss it after you graduate."

"Maybe you don't miss being here, but I've got a pretty good life going for me, so I definitely will," she said as she leaned away from his car. "Anyway, you'd better be here to talk about Tristan and Ava. Otherwise, Mom is not going to be happy."

She crossed her arms in silent judgment as Elliott rolled up the windows and got out of his car.

"Well, lucky for her, what I need to talk about kind of goes along with that whole situation, so…"

"Oh?" she asked. Elliott raised his eyebrows at her and he felt a blush rise to his cheeks as he thought about her again. She quickly realized he was talking about finding his soulmate, and the biggest smile spread across her freckled face. "OH!"

"Yeah." He looked away, embarrassed, ruffling the back of his hair.

"Oh, I wanna hear all the juicy details!" She started bouncing up and down as her friend Emily pulled up behind them.

"Yo, Lucy! You ready to go?" she shouted from the driver's seat.

Lucy waved at her before giving Elliott a disappointed look.

"You WILL be giving me all the details when I get back!"

she said, pointing a finger in his face before turning around and walking towards Emily's car.

"If I'm even still here when you get back!" he yelled at her teasingly.

"You'd better be!" she shouted back as she hopped into the car.

Elliott watched them drive away, waving at his sister before turning back towards the house. His mother was stepping out onto the wrap-around porch, no doubt drawn outside by the shouting. Her usual light brown waves of hair seemed messy and unbrushed, and she had dark circles under her eyes, as if she hadn't slept in days.

"Elliott!" she said as he walked over to give her a hug. "You should have told me you were coming over. I would have made something for you to eat!"

"It was kind of a last-minute decision," he said, stepping inside the house. "And besides, I don't need you worrying about me. You look like you've been through enough already."

She sighed as she shut the front door. "It's been... hard for all of us recently."

"How is Tristan doing? I haven't really heard anything since the funeral."

"He's... well..." She trailed off, trying her best not to make eye contact as they walked through the house and into the kitchen.

It was a beautiful kitchen with sparkling white marble countertops, large enough to have plenty of counter space, and an island sitting right in the center of the room. A large window of glass with a sliding door that led into the vast back yard sat at the back of the room, with a smaller table in front of it for less formal occasions where they didn't need to use the dining room.

"Mom, what is it?" he said, leaning on the counter of the center island.

She opened her mouth to speak and then closed it again.

"Mom?"

"I'm sorry. It's just a little hard to describe," she said, busying herself with getting out a bowl of pretzels to put on the kitchen counter.

"Describe?"

"Well... you've never made the bond, which makes it difficult to explain."

"The bond?" Elliott rolled his eyes. "Mom, come on, what difference would that make? It's not like you have, and you and Phil are perfectly happy together."

"You know regular love and the bond that comes from... well, THE Bond are very different," she said, pacing as she picked at her fingernails.

"Just call it what it is, Mom. A soulmate. And I am aware just how different they are."

She stopped pacing and looked at him, walking back over to the center island.

"Fine then. When your soulmate"—she put emphasis on the word—"is ripped apart from you, it can be pretty traumatizing."

"Well, yeah, obviously. Pretty sure humans are traumatized by death, too," Elliott said, popping a pretzel into his mouth.

"You know it's different than that!" she said with an exasperated tone. "It's like a piece of you died along with them."

"Yeah, Mom, I know. I was at the funeral, remember? I saw what her death did to him. I was just kidding around."

She gave a deep sigh. "I know, I know. Poorly timed humor has always been how you coped." She rubbed her forehead. "I just wish you had been here. Tristan really could have used his brother during all of this."

"I'm sorry, Mom, I just... I couldn't be here anymore. Not with Dad looming around every corner just waiting to ruin my life, or worse, someone else's because of me. And it didn't quite seem like Tristan wanted me around after the funeral, anyway."

"I understand that, but still..." She looked down at the countertop sadly. "I couldn't stand to lose another child."

He put his hand on top of hers for comfort. His family had

already lost so much, even before Ava's death. He was too young to remember when it happened, but he saw the look on his mother's face whenever she passed that photo of *her* in the dining room.

"I'm here now, Mom. Please, just... tell me what happened to Tristan."

"Human life was too hard without Ava, so he... he turned... and never came back."

Elliott tried to comprehend what his mother had said. "What do you mean, he never came back?"

"Elliott... he's stuck as a wolf. Permanently."

"So, have you thought about finding that guy after your weird interaction in the hallway?" Thea asked as she and Mia made their way back to their dorm.

"I haven't really thought about him, to be honest."

It wasn't an entire lie. She had played that interaction in her head again to figure out just what had happened with him, so it wasn't like she was thinking about him specifically. And she certainly wasn't looking for him. At least, not until Thea mentioned it.

"You liar," she said with a cheeky grin.

"Am not! You just put the idea in my head. And you know, maybe if I found him, I could ask him what all that weird staring was about."

"I'd just kinda like to stare at him again, to be honest."

Mia gave her a dirty look. "You shouldn't sound so shallow, Thea. Looks aren't everything."

"Shallow? No, Mia, you misunderstand me. I'm an artist and I just enjoy looking at good art."

Mia let out a loud laugh. "People aren't art, Thea!"

"But they are the subject of many pieces of art," Thea said, pointing a finger at her.

"I guess," Mia said as they walked up to the tall dorm building. "Still kinda shallow, though." She swiped her student ID, and the doors to the building popped open.

Thea just laughed as they walked into the lobby. "Okay, okay."

The lounge to the left of the entrance held a couple of couches and a ping-pong table where some students were milling around, but it was mostly quiet otherwise. As they walked past the front desk and toward the elevators, the assistant gave them a wave.

"So, I was thinking, maybe we should go out tonight?" Thea said as they pushed the up button and waited for the elevator.

"Go out? Thea, it's Monday."

"Not like party 'go out,' just get off campus for a bit. Maybe we could go to the mall for dinner!"

"You'd rather have food court food instead of dining hall food?"

"Is there really a difference? I just think we could use some time off campus."

The elevator gave a ding as the doors opened, and they got on and pushed the button for the fourth floor.

"I suppose you're right. We did kind of hole ourselves up in our room after the whole Friday night party thing."

"Exactly! And who knows, maybe you'll see someone there." She nudged her elbow into Mia's arm.

"Of course that's what you're actually thinking about! Why is it always boys with you? And you know what, I'm kind of having déjà vu from Friday night now. Weren't you saying something about meeting someone then? And how did that play out?"

"Uh..." She could not come up with the words as the elevator dinged once more, and the doors opened to let them out. "Anyway... What really matters is that I'm going to get some good burgers for once, instead of the crap they call burgers here."

Mia rolled her eyes as they made their way down the hallway towards their room. "I'm pretty sure food court burgers are just as bad as dining hall burgers."

"That, my friend, is where you are wrong," Thea said as they walked into their room.

"Whatever you say. I guess I'll just have to take your word for it." Mia shrugged as she tossed her backpack into her desk chair.

She grabbed her laptop from her desk and brought it over to her bed.

"Mia, what are you doing?" Thea asked.

"Uh, gonna play a quick round of Duel of Ages?"

"But we were going to the mall."

"Oh, you meant, like, now?"

"Well, yeah, we can shop a bit first!"

Mia put her laptop back down on her desk with a sigh. "I suppose I can play later then."

"You sure will!" Thea said, grabbing her purse and heading for the door.

Mia grabbed her wallet and followed her outside.

Mia watched as Thea sank her teeth into quite possibly the biggest burger she had ever seen. She looked like she was in heaven the way she savored every bite, and it kind of made Mia wish she had gotten one too, instead of a lousy chicken caesar wrap.

"Well, is it everything you've ever dreamed of and more?" Mia asked.

She was kind of glad they came to the mall. It was rather quiet because it was a Monday night, compared to how loud the dining halls got with the gossip and hustle and bustle of the students coming in and out. It was refreshing.

"Oh, 'and more' is definitely the answer," Thea said between bites. "And you are totally jealous you didn't get one!"

"You're right; however, I'm not the one that's going to be

dealing with heartburn later because of it."

"Fair point." She took another bite of the burger. It was almost halfway gone already. "However, you're really missing out."

"Whatever you say, Thea," Mia said, finishing up her wrap.

"So, we gonna do any more shopping after this?" Thea asked as she finished the last of her burger and started on her fries.

"I'd kind of rather get back and start on some homework. Besides, I don't have a lot of money to just blow through on random junk from the mall, and you've already gotten enough."

"Random junk?" Thea exclaimed. "I think you're exaggerating a bit. Clothes are not random junk."

"Yeah, you say that, till you end up buying more than just clothes."

"Ugh, fine. You're probably right, anyway."

They both quickly finished eating and headed towards the escalators. They were about halfway down when they heard a commotion from behind them.

"'Scuse me!" A young girl with light brown hair tied up in pigtails was rushing down the stairs of the escalator. "Sorry!" she said to every person she snuck by.

"Wonder what's got her in such a hurry," Thea said.

"Sorry again!" she said as she flew by Mia and Thea just as they reached the bottom of the escalator.

The two made their way outside to the parking lot just as the sun was going down. The girl that pushed her way down the escalator was already halfway across the parking lot when they saw her trip over a patch of raised gravel and fall fast to the pavement. She hit the ground hard and skidded a few feet. It had to have been one of the worst wipeouts Mia had ever seen.

"Oh my gosh!" Thea exclaimed, running as fast as she could towards her.

Mia could hardly keep up with her and was out of breath by the time she reached them. Just how did she get to the middle of the parking lot so fast in the first place?

"Are... you... okay?" Mia said between breaths.

Thea held her hand out to help the girl up, and when she stood, there was nothing but dirt on her. No scrapes or blood. How was that possible?

"Oh yeah, I'm fine!" the girl said, wiping the gravel off of her dress. "I've taken worse falls than that before! It looks like you could use a little help, though," she said to Mia, giggling a bit at her lack of breath.

"I'll be fine, just need to catch my breath," Mia said.

"Yeah, she's not really a runner," Thea said.

"I can see that." The girl chuckled again, and something about her felt really familiar. "Anyway, thanks for your help, but I gotta get going before my ride leaves out of boredom. I've already made her wait long enough. See ya!"

She continued to run to a car parked a few lanes away. Her ride must not have seen her fall. Mia couldn't imagine she would just let her friend lie there on the ground.

"All right, Mia, let's get going!" Thea said.

Mia watched as the car drove away, leaving her looking at the woods beyond the lot. For a second, she could swear she saw a big brown wolf staring at her. She squinted her eyes, not believing what she was seeing. Its golden eyes bore into her, and she couldn't look away.

"Mia?"

She quickly glanced at Thea. "Yeah, I'm coming."

When she turned to look back at the wolf, it was gone.

CHAPTER SIX

AVA'S FUNERAL FLASHED THROUGH Elliott's head. Seeing her body lying so still in that coffin unsettled him. Her short black hair that normally stuck up in various directions sat gelled down and straight. It framed her face in a way that looked awkward and not Ava-like. They did a beautiful painting of makeup on her face, something he had never seen on his sister-in-law before. She was almost unrecognizable, and she was still. So still. He could only guess how his brother must have felt seeing her like this.

Tristan, normally so strong and full of life, the true Alpha to their pack, crumpled in the face of his soulmate's death. His dark brown hair had grown to his shoulders, unkempt despite the formality of the funeral, and it seemed like he hadn't shaved in weeks as the stubble on his chin had grown out of control.

His brown eyes were cold and dark as Elliott watched strangers tell him how sorry they were for his loss as they exited the church. He didn't think his brother was even paying attention to them when he would nod and give an absentminded thanks.

It was like his brother was stuck in a place far away from here, and Elliott was afraid he'd never return.

Elliott walked over to his brother and placed a concerned hand on his shoulder. "Hey, Tris."

Tristan's head lifted to look at Elliott. His eyes were glazed over, and being this close, he could see that his brother hadn't been sleeping. The dark circles under his eyes were deep. It broke his heart to see his brother like this.

"How're you holding up?" Elliott asked.

Tristan looked at him without a word, but it was all Elliott needed to see to give him his answer. Anguish filled his face, and he could feel Tristan's anger radiating off his body in waves.

"I'm sorry, that was a dumb question," Elliott said, looking down at his shoes to avoid his brother's icy gaze.

They stood there silently next to each other for a while before Tristan finally spoke.

"Where have you been?" Tristan whispered, his voice raspy.

Elliott wasn't sure if it was the lack of talking, or if his brother had been crying so much he lost his voice, but it broke his heart to hear. He swallowed the lump that was rising in his throat and dared to look up at his brother, only to see that he was staring off into the distance.

"What do you mean?" Elliott asked.

"I've hardly seen you these past three years. Where have you been that you think you can just walk back into this family like nothing ever happened?" Tristan turned on him, anger swelling in his voice. "Just because Ava died doesn't mean you can just pretend like you didn't leave us all behind. If you were with us that night, maybe things would've gone differently!" He looked at Elliott with a fierceness that made him tremble.

The sudden outburst confused Elliott. Where was all of this coming from?

"Tristan, that's not really fair—"

"No, you know what's not fair? That the love of my life is dead, and you just get to run away back to your nice perfect life and forget about all of this like it never happened."

Tristan's words stung. Elliott had never heard his brother say anything so harsh to him. If this was how he truly felt, how come he'd never said anything?

"Tris, I—"

"I don't want to hear it, Elliott," he said, walking out of the church.

He wished he'd known sooner how Tristan felt about his absence from Elk Grove. He would've come back. He could've spent more time with them if he only knew how much hurt his absence had caused.

He was angry at Tristan for keeping all of this inside. For blowing up at him now, instead of just talking like adults. But he was more angry at himself for ignoring his family for the last three years. He couldn't even blame Tristan for acting this way.

Elliott walked out of the church, and Tristan was nowhere to be seen. A moment later, he heard a sad howl in the distance. Tristan had shifted.

That was the last time he had seen his brother.

Elliott regretted not chasing him down after their argument. Instead, he just went back to his car and drove all the way back home without saying a word to his family. Now he'd probably never see his brother again, at least in human form.

"Honey, are you all right?" Elliott's mom chimed in, drawing him out of his thoughts.

"Sorry, I was just… thinking about Ava's funeral."

His mother looked at him sadly.

"Elliott, it's not your fault. You know that, right?" She reached across the counter and placed her hand comfortingly on his. "You can't blame yourself for what your brother has done."

"Can't I, though?" He pulled his hand away and started pacing. "The last thing he said to me was that maybe if I had been here during that full moon, we could have saved Ava."

"And how would your presence have saved her, Elliott? She was driven off the road, far away from where we even were. None of us could have stopped it."

"I don't know, but…" He blinked back the tears that were forming in his eyes as he turned away towards the counter. He didn't want to show this sort of weakness in front of anyone, not even his mom. "But Tristan seemed to think so, and now he's gone too!"

"Tristan was speaking from a place of hurt, and I'd bet now that he's got a clearer head, he would take back what he said in an instant. Your brother isn't gone, Elliott. He's just changed. And we'll change him back. Now that you're back, we can—"

A pounding on the front door cut her off.

"Yo, Elliott!" a voice called from the front of the house as the thumping continued.

Elliott and his mother shared a look before he got up and headed to the front door. Opening it, his roommate Zeke was standing on the front porch, fist still hanging in the air as he was getting ready to knock once again.

"Zeke, careful with the front door, man. It sounded like you were about to break it down." Zeke looked utterly exhausted, like he had run here from all the way across town. His black faux hawk was sticking up in strange places, and Elliott was sure he saw a bead of sweat forming on his forehead.

"Well, sorry," he said sarcastically. "You sounded real urgent on the phone!" He crossed his arms, annoyed.

The phone call! Elliott was so caught up in talking about Tristan, he'd completely forgotten why he'd come here in the first place.

"Dude, that was, like, hours ago."

"Well, I'm here now." He gestured to the doorway for Elliott to step aside so he could come in.

"Sorry, come on in. I didn't mean to keep you standing out there on the porch."

Zeke sighed as if he was inconvenienced by having to come all the way here, and he stepped inside. Elliott showed him the way to the kitchen, Zeke stopping once by the mirror in the hallway to fix his hair back into the faux hawk he always kept so neat.

Elliott's mother had fixed herself a cup of tea while he was gone and was checking the text messages on her phone. Hearing them walk in, she looked up with a smile to greet them.

"Hey there, Mrs. C, nice place you got here," Zeke said, smiling while he took in the enormous kitchen.

"Nice to see you again too, Ezekiel," his mother said, smirking at the knowledge that Zeke's full name would upset him.

Zeke cringed, and his smile slowly faded. "It's just Zeke, actually," he said without a hint of emotion.

"Oh, I know," she said, her grin growing wider as she took a sip of her tea.

Elliott couldn't help but let a small smirk slip onto his face, knowing that his mother enjoyed teasing his best friend. At least the mood had been lightened a bit from their somber conversation before.

"So, what is it that brings you here so urgently that you almost broke down my front door?" she asked.

"Okay, you two are really exaggerating how hard I was knocking," Zeke said as he took off his leather jacket and threw it over a chair by the island.

"Yeah, that's not what it sounded like in here," Elliott said, patting him on the back and offering him the seat he threw his jacket on.

He sat down and absentmindedly pulled out his phone. Elliott and his mother shared a look of confusion.

Elliott rolled his eyes at his roommate's short attention span.

"Uh, Zeke?"

"What?" he said, looking up from his phone, confused.

"Are you going to tell us why you're here or not?" Elliott's mother asked.

"Oh, didn't Elliott already tell you? I assumed that's why he came over here. I actually am eager to hear all the details myself—"

"Oh, just spit it out, Zeke!" His mother absolutely hated the way Zeke would ramble on about things instead of getting straight to the point. Elliott enjoyed that aspect of him. It made him fun to live with sometimes.

"Well, if you didn't tell her, I don't think I should be the one to. It is your big news, after all, right, Elliott?" Zeke said, placing his phone on the counter and drumming his hands in anticipation.

"News? What news, Elliott? I thought you came over here to discuss your brother?" she asked, concerned.

"I'm sorry, Mom, you just wanted to get straight to the point. I completely forgot what I actually came here to talk to you about," he said, rubbing the back of his head nervously.

"Well then, let's hear—"

A bang came from the living room as Lucy burst through the front door. "Did I miss it? Don't say another word until I get in there, Elliott! I wanna hear the entire story from start to finish!" she yelled as he heard her taking her shoes off to drop them by the front door.

"Does everyone know about this 'big news' but me?" his mom questioned, offended.

"Okay, I'm here!" Lucy said, practically running into the room. Her dress was torn at the bottom, and her knees were brown with dirt. "Oh, hey, Zeke."

"Hey, twerp." He nodded in her direction.

She scoffed at him and turned towards Elliott. "So, did I miss all the details? I wanna hear all about her! What's she like? What was it like? Tristan would never tell me anything, so that means you've gotta tell me everything!" She was bouncing with joy and staring at Elliott anxiously.

"Whoa, slow down, Lu, I haven't mentioned anything at all!" He put his arms up defensively as he backed away from her.

"A girl? Elliott? Did you meet your soulmate?" his mother said, astonished.

"Oh, man, did I ruin the surprise?" Lucy said, pouting, knowing that she had spoiled the news.

Elliott sighed, taking a seat next to Zeke. "It's fine, Lucy, now everyone knows. And that's that..." He trailed off, not sure what else to say.

"What do you mean 'and that's that'? Isn't there more?" Lucy prodded.

"Give him time, Lucy. You know your brother isn't one to get wrapped up in feelings," his mother said, taking another sip of her tea as she leaned back on the counter.

"Whoa, wait, hold up. You met a girl?" Zeke said. "And you didn't tell your best friend first? That's cold."

"I didn't—I just—Ugh!" Elliott groaned, standing up to pace again while trying to think of the right words to say. "I don't... I don't want anything to do with her! That's why I didn't think you needed to hear it first. I wasn't going to tell Lucy—she just found out through her stupid sisterly intuition. I really only came here to see how I could avoid this stupid 'mate' thing altogether!"

The three of them looked at him like he had lost his mind. They would never understand why he would want to avoid her. The only one who truly would was Tristan, and he was gone.

"What do you mean..." his mother said, setting down her mug and pushing away from the counter. "You want nothing to do with her?" She looked angry as she walked towards him, arms crossed in that disappointed, motherly way.

"I... I don't want this. That's all." He backed up towards the kitchen table and looked away, unable to keep eye contact with his mother.

"How can you throw away something so precious?" Lucy

chimed in. "Most werewolves wait their whole lives to find their soulmate, and you're going to just toss that away?"

"Could you two just please... think about this from my perspective?" Elliott said, exasperated.

His mother and Lucy opened their mouths to protest once again, but Zeke cut them off.

"I get it, man," he said in a serious tone.

"You do?" Elliott asked.

"It's your dad," he said, standing up and walking to the middle of the room. "You're afraid of what he might do to her, just like what he did to Ava. Right?"

Elliott's mother and Lucy looked at each other, and then back to Elliott sheepishly. They knew they were in the wrong for coming after him.

"So it's not that you don't want to be with her..." Zeke continued. "It's that you want to protect her. That's part of the mate thing, right? The need to protect?"

"I guess it is," Elliott said, not willing to look at anyone in the room. His cheeks flushed at the thought of the need to protect this girl he didn't know. Everything about the mate bond was embarrassing to him.

"I'm so sorry, sweetheart," his mother said, walking over to hug him. "These past few months have been so hard on all of us. We shouldn't be giving you more grief just because you want to protect someone from your father."

"Yeah, sorry, E, I wasn't thinking," Lucy mumbled.

"So, what're you gonna do then?" Zeke asked.

"I guess I could just... try to avoid her?"

"Isn't that campus, like, tiny, though?" Lucy asked. "It's gonna be hard to ignore her. And besides, I don't think you should ignore this just because your dad might do something bad."

"He literally killed Ava," Zeke said.

"We don't know that for sure!" Lucy said.

"There was actually some pretty convincing evidence that the 'accident' was no accident," Zeke argued back.

"Says who?" Lucy asked.

"Okay, enough!" Elliott's mom shouted. "This isn't about Ava, so just drop it. And Lucy, this is your brother's decision, not yours."

"But—"

"But nothing, young lady. He's made his decision, and it's final." She turned back to Elliott. "If you think you can avoid this girl, then fine, but don't be surprised if things don't go your way. She's your mate for a reason, and fate will see to it that you're together in the end."

Avoiding the girl proved to be more difficult than Elliott thought it would be. It seemed like every corner he turned, she was there. It really must have been a miracle that they hadn't met before that day.

He started making a mental note of every place he saw her throughout the week, just so he could avoid going near there at those specific times. But it never seemed to work. He couldn't understand why, but even with his best efforts to memorize where she should be every day, he wound up running into her somewhere else.

He felt as if she was teasing him, like she knew what he was doing, so she would change up her path to class just on the off chance of accidentally running into him.

He practically sighed with relief once the week ended. If just one week was this uncomfortable, how the hell was he supposed to avoid her for the rest of the school year?

Come the second week, he made a big mistake. As he was walking through the quad towards his car, he caught her eye. She immediately changed direction and started walking towards him with great ferocity. Panicking, Elliott made a beeline towards the nearest building. Not his best idea ever, given how awkward it made him look, but it worked in a pinch. Though if she didn't realize he was avoiding her before, she definitely did now.

He found himself in the campus library and quickly searched for a place to hide. Luckily, the shelves full of books provided brilliant cover for that sort of thing. He hid behind a shelf facing the entrance, where he could easily peek between the books to see if she had followed him inside.

Of course, with his luck, she walked in shortly after he had found his hiding spot. She looked back and forth at the other students in the library, and a look of disappointment crossed her face when she didn't see him. His heart dropped in his chest to see her so upset, and to know he caused it all. It tore him apart inside.

She pulled her phone out of her pocket with a huff and sighed after staring at it. She then turned around and left the building, no doubt having no time to pursue him any further.

He was extremely lucky that she didn't have the time to chase him down. But even though he ran away from her, another part of him wanted to follow her, the mate bond messing with him once again.

He felt bad that he forced her to chase him in here, especially since it made him look guilty of avoiding her. He could have just faked a phone call or pretended he forgot something. Now she was probably wondering what she did that made him act this way, and he felt horrible.

If only she could know why he treated her this way. Maybe one day when his father was out of the picture she would, but who knew if that day would ever come.

CHAPTER SEVEN

"HE TOOK ONE LOOK at me and ran straight into the library!" Mia exclaimed to Thea as she paced around their room.

"Tell me you followed him, though," Thea said, looking at Mia over the painting she was working on at her desk.

"Of course I did! But as soon as I got in there, it's like he disappeared!" She sat down at her desk in defeat. "He was probably just hiding behind the nearest bookshelf."

"You didn't check?"

"I was gonna be late for class if I scoured the entire building." She leaned on her desk and stared at her open textbook and the notes she was taking before Thea came back from class.

"That's just too bad." Thea went back to her painting. "Because if that were me, I totally would've said, 'Screw class, I'm finding this boy!'"

"That's the difference between you and me, I guess."

"Electives are overrated anyway. Just glide through 'em, earning the minimum passing grade. It's not like they do anything for you in your major, anyway." Thea shrugged.

Mia looked down at the notes she was taking on the latest chapter of her European History textbook.

"Yeah… sure…"

Thea just laughed, and Mia went back to her note-taking. Or, at least she attempted to, but her mind kept wandering back to that boy again, as it had all week.

"I've got it!" Thea suddenly shouted.

Mia jumped, and when she looked back down at her notes, she saw a huge line across the page she was writing on.

"Thea!" She groaned.

"Sorry, I just had an idea," she said, placing her paintbrush down and turning to face Mia.

"About what?"

"Your boy problem!"

Mia rolled her eyes. "Oh, here we go." She put her pencil down and turned her chair towards Thea. She waved her on to prattle off her conspiracy.

"What if he's just playing hard to get?"

Mia blinked at her. "Hard to get? Thea, did you miss the part where I said he took one look at my face and then ran?"

"No, I heard you, but hear me out." She got up and walked between them towards the windows. "What if he wanted you to follow him? Maybe he was playing a little game of cat and mouse, but he didn't expect you to be late for class." She turned around to face Mia and pointed at her. "Huh? How's that for a theory?"

Thea stood triumphantly in front of her, as if she'd just cracked the case wide open. Mia stared at her in disbelief.

"Well? Say something!" Thea said after a solid minute of silence had gone by.

"You've officially lost it." She chuckled and turned back towards her desk.

"Oh, come on! That could totally be it." She threw her hands in the air before crossing them in front of her defensively.

"I'd have a better time believing he just conveniently

remembered he needed something in the library at the same time he saw me than 'he was playing hard to get.'"

"Well, maybe that's it then. He just remembered he needed something," Thea said, sitting back down at her desk.

"Yeah..." Mia stared at her textbook absentmindedly for a moment. "I still think he's just avoiding me."

"Oh, come on, Mia!" she yelled, standing back up again. "Why's it so hard to believe it was just a coincidence?"

"Why's it so hard to believe it wasn't?"

"Because... well..."

Mia raised her eyebrows at Thea, waiting for her to come up with a good reason.

"Because you are a wonderful and gorgeous person, and you've done nothing to that boy to make him avoid you?"

Mia let out a laugh. "You really are something else sometimes."

"And I mean it too, you know! That boy has no reason to dislike you, and if he does, I'll personally track him down and fight him for you."

"That's good to know." Mia chuckled. "But how about for now we just leave it alone and get back to the work we're supposed to be doing?" She gestured between her notes and Thea's painting.

"Ugh, fine," Thea said, walking back over to her desk. "But next time you see him, you chase him down and find out what's wrong with him. Got it?"

"Yeah, yeah, I will," Mia said sarcastically.

Though the more she thought about it, the more she figured Thea was right. She wanted to talk to him and figure out what was going on with this whole situation. Or maybe she just wanted to see him again...

Butterflies fluttered in her stomach, and she tried to push them down. She did not have a crush on this boy; she couldn't. She didn't know him, and he was clearly avoiding her. Even if she did like him, it was a doomed crush. Just like every other one she'd had in her life.

Saturday morning arrived and Mia sat at her desk, attempting to write a short story for one of her classes. The cursor on her laptop blinked on the blank white background of her word document, but no inspiration was coming to her.

She leaned back in her chair and groaned, placing her hands over her eyes and rubbing them. She couldn't focus on anything with her mind still trying to figure out why this boy would be avoiding her. No matter how many times Thea had tried to convince her she was just overreacting, she couldn't believe it.

"What are you groaning about over there?" Thea said groggily from her bed.

"Sorry, I didn't mean to wake you up," Mia said, looking across the room at Thea.

"Naw you didn't—" She was cut off by a yawn. "I've been up for a while now."

"Oh yeah? Could've fooled me," Mia said.

"So, what is it you're groaning about this time?"

Mia stared back at her blank computer screen, the blinking cursor taunting her once again. "I can't think of anything to write about for my class."

"Homework already? On a Saturday morning?"

"We've been over this a thousand times, Thea. I like to get my work done early."

"Yeah, well, it sounds like your brain doesn't like that idea. Maybe you should go back to bed. Dreams are always good inspiration, you know."

"Thea, it's like…" Mia looked at the clock on the corner of her laptop screen. "It's already 11:30. I am not going back to bed."

"Suit yourself." Thea yawned again and rolled back over to scroll through her phone.

Mia got up and went to her bedside table to grab her journal out from the drawer. Thea had a good point about dreams being a source of inspiration. Maybe there was something in her dream journal that could help.

"What's that?" Thea asked, suddenly curious about what she was doing.

"It's a dream journal. Sometimes when I have dreams that could make good stories, I write them down in here."

"Ah, so taking my advice then," Thea said with a tired smile.

"In a way, I guess. We'll see if there's anything even good in here." She flipped through the pages, reading idea after idea, but nothing really jumped out at her. Every time something seemed like it could be good, she would immediately dismiss it as something that would require too much development to be a short story.

With a huff, she tossed her journal back into the drawer and shut it. "Nothing useful for this assignment, of course." She leaned back on her bed and continued to be plagued by thoughts of why that boy would hate her so much that he would be actively avoiding her.

After he ran away from her on Wednesday, she hadn't seen him at all. Normally she happened upon him by chance, like something inside her told her to take a different route to class and there he was, but she didn't have that at all in these last few days. She continued to stare down at the campus from her window, her mind running in thousands of tiny circles.

"Mia?"

"Hm?" She turned to look at Thea, who was staring at her.

"I asked if you were okay?"

"Oh. Uh, yeah. I just need to clear my head, that's all." Mia walked over to the door and put her shoes on. Maybe a walk around town would help her out.

"Where are you going?" Thea sat up in her bed.

"Out for a walk."

"Without me?" she said, offended, as she got out of bed and started getting dressed.

"Apparently not." Mia rolled her eyes and smiled.

CHAPTER EIGHT

"THIS ISN'T THE USUAL way to the café," Thea said as she followed Mia down the sidewalk.

"I know. I just figured we could use a bit of a change in scenery for once," Mia said, looking at all the different shop windows they'd never passed by before. "And who knows, maybe I'll find something inspiring. Or maybe there's a cute thrift shop for you to find some new clothes to upscale or something."

"Hm, I suppose you're right. A new path is always fun, like an adventure!" she said, skipping along the sidewalk with glee.

"Sure, like an adventure." Mia trailed off, her mind wandering as she let her instincts lead her along the path. She wasn't exactly sure what pulled her to go in a different direction than usual, but she felt like she needed to walk down this street instead of their usual one. It was close to the same feeling she got on campus whenever she would run into that boy, and deep down, it excited her.

They came upon a beautiful shop window at the corner of the street. It was filled with beautiful crystals and glistening dark fabric. There was a book open on a magnificent wooden pedestal in the middle of the setup, and a black backdrop that twinkled with LED lights. The words on the book's pages were written in beautiful calligraphy, with detailed illustrations to go along with it.

"Wow! That's so pretty," Thea said as she examined the window.

"It's very different," Mia stated, unsure of what to think of such a peculiar window display. The page it was open to contained a description of fairies, and a spell with how to summon one. Just what kind of shop was this?

"We definitely have to go in!" Thea said as she dragged Mia towards the door.

"Oh, okay," she said as Thea pulled her inside.

Little bells chimed as they walked into the store, and the inside was even more beautiful than what they saw outside. Colorful fabrics were draped across the ceiling, with twinkle lights spread throughout them to make it seem like tiny stars were dancing on the ceiling.

Lavish bookshelves lined the walls with novels that looked almost ancient, overflowing from their shelves. Displays of incense and crystals sat on tables throughout the store, along with an entire wall of various ingredients up by the registers.

Many candles were lit at various tables, giving the entire room a magical and inviting feel. The scent of lavender filled the room, bringing a wave of calmness that made Mia feel like she could stay there forever.

"Oh, it's like a little witchy shop!" Thea exclaimed, interrupting Mia's train of thought as she tried to observe and make a note of everything in the room.

Thea made her way over to the tarot stand and picked up a deck, examining the back of it while Mia started scanning the books on the shelves. Many of them were of spells and rituals, others history and folklore from all over the world. She picked up a book and skimmed through it quickly; it was about werewolves, their history, and how they lived. She couldn't help but chuckle to herself as she put it back on the shelf. Just how many people were actually interested in this kind of thing?

Looking around the store, she suddenly noticed that she and Thea were the only ones there. She didn't even see an employee around.

"Thea, where is everyone?" she said, walking over to the Tarot setup Thea was looking at.

Thea looked around and shrugged. "That is kind of weird. Maybe they're just in the back?" She nodded towards a doorway behind the registers. Colorful beads hung there to keep it separate from the store. "Hello?" she shouted towards the doorway. "Is anyone in there?"

They heard a bang followed by the crash of something falling to the ground. "Uh, just a moment, if you please!" a lovely voice shouted back.

Mia and Thea looked at each other in concern. "Are you all right? Do you need any help?" Mia shouted back at her.

"No, no! I'm fine! Thank you for the concern." They heard glass clinking together before a girl suddenly popped her head out through the beads. "So sorry to keep you waiting like that. Things are a little hectic right now," she said, while wiping what looked like dirt off on her brown apron.

She was absolutely gorgeous. Long auburn waves of hair framed her face, which was done up in professional quality makeup, complete with black lipstick and a dark green smokey eye. She wore many piercings in her ears, and her bright green eyes were striking against her pale freckled face.

"So, what can I do for you?" she said, her voice ringing sweetly in Mia's ears.

"Oh, we were just passing by and couldn't help but be curious about your shop," Thea said.

"Well, of course! Feel free to take a look around, and if you have any questions, please ask!" She gestured to the rest of the shop. "I'm always happy to help anyone with an interest in the world's magic." She smiled sweetly at them.

"Will do, uh…" Thea looked to see if the girl was wearing a name tag but crossed her arms and huffed when she couldn't find one.

"Oh! I'm sorry, my name is Nixie."

"It's nice to meet you, Nixie!" Thea offered out her hand, and Nixie shook it. "So… do you do readings here?" she said, picking up a Tarot deck off the nearest table. "My friend over there could really use some insight, I think."

Mia looked sheepishly at her, wishing Thea would leave her out of whatever scheme she was planning.

"Unfortunately, not right now. My parents, the owners of this store, are away dealing with a family emergency, and my mother is the one that's good with divination. I'm not super confident in my ability to read the cards accurately. I mostly deal with growing our herbs for potions and cooking." She shrugged and picked at her nails nervously.

"Hm, well, that's too bad," Thea said, putting the deck back on the table.

"We have plenty of books on the subject, though, if you were interested in learning how to do readings yourself."

Thea thought about that a moment before deciding against it. "Is there anything that could help with writer's block?"

"Writer's block?" Nixie asked, confused.

"Thea!" Mia said, shuffling over to her. "She does not need to be bothered by my lame problems."

Nixie looked deep in thought. "I suppose we have some crystals that could bring about clarity to help with a creativity block…" she mumbled to herself before realizing Mia was talking to her. "Oh! It's not a problem at all. People come in here looking for help with things all the time! Even if they don't fully believe it will work, they still try. In fact, most people are drawn to our shop without even realizing it!"

"That's… interesting," Thea mumbled, not entirely believing

Nixie's words.

"I guess that does make me feel a bit better then…" Mia said.

"Now what were you saying about crystals again?" Thea chimed in.

Nixie showed them to a part of the store filled with crystals of all shapes and sizes, and before they knew it, both Mia and Thea had picked out a few to take home.

"Thank you so much," Mia said.

"No problem at all. Thank you both for stopping in!" She handed them their crystals in beautiful velvet bags. "I hope those crystals can really help you out, and don't be strangers. I would love to chat with you two again sometime! And maybe when my parents are back, you can get yourself that reading," Nixie said, winking at her as they all made their way to the front door.

"Will do! See ya around, Nixie!" Thea called as they walked through the door. Mia chuckled. Thea always found it so easy to make friends wherever they went.

When they stepped out onto the steps of the shop, light droplets of rain had begun to fall. The two shielded themselves under the awning above the shop's door.

"Aw, man, I didn't bring an umbrella," Mia said, frowning.

"The café isn't far. We could make a run for it." Thea shrugged.

"You know how I feel about running."

"Well, it's either that or take a slow walk and get even more wet," Thea said, crossing her arms defiantly.

Mia rolled her eyes at her. "You're not wrong, but still…"

"Okay, on three!" Thea said, ignoring Mia's distaste in the idea. "One… two… three… go!"

Thea sprinted off as fast as she could, leaving Mia standing there.

She groaned. "Well, I guess I have no choice now." She started running, nowhere near as fast as Thea had before. It was an awkward and slow run, and she was putting all of her effort into not slipping on the wet pavement.

She made it to the café two whole minutes after Thea had, her breath catching in her throat as she tried hard not to choke on the phlegm that always came up when she ran.

"After you, loser of the race," Thea said, bowing dramatically and extending her hand towards the café as Mia stood there, still trying to catch her breath.

Mia laughed. "Yeah, yeah, gimmie a minute." She huffed one more time and got herself together before making her way up the small set of steps towards the door.

"You know..." Mia said as she turned to look at Thea after reaching for the door handle. "One of these days, I might just beat you!"

"Yeah, in your dreams!" Thea laughed.

Mia pulled open the door and turned to walk inside. As she did, someone else was attempting to leave, and she ran straight into their chest. Caught off guard, she fell backwards.

The boy grabbed her arm and yanked her back upwards before she got very far. Looking up to see who it was, she made direct eye contact with the very boy who was avoiding her.

Her heart started beating faster in her chest, and the butterflies came back to her stomach once again. She swallowed hard and tried to shove her feelings back down, but she could feel her face heating with a blush.

His eyes seemed to grow wide as he realized who had run into him, and a flush came to his cheeks.

"A-are you okay?" he stuttered.

"Yeah, I think so," Mia said, pushing her glasses back up and getting her bearings. "But we've really gotta stop bumping into each other like this."

CHAPTER NINE

THE JOKE JUST SLIPPED out, and Mia immediately put her hands over her mouth. 'We've really got to stop bumping into each other like this'? What kind of line was that? She felt like she could die from embarrassment herself any second, and it didn't help that she heard Thea chuckling behind her. Maybe it was her turn to just run away and act like nothing even happened.

As she was considering her best options, she saw the boy was actually grinning at her joke, which only made her blush even more.

This boy's smile could light up an entire room, and Mia's heart skipped a few beats looking at him. She tried to bury those feelings again as soon as they rose up. There was no use in pining for a boy who was trying to avoid her like the plague.

"Are you gonna actually walk out the door or not, Elliott?" a young girl's voice said, breaking the awkward tension the two were having. Mia hadn't realized until that moment that the two of them were blocking the entrance.

"Yeah, sorry, Lucy," Elliott said, gesturing for them to walk down the steps.

Mia walked back towards Thea, who was just standing there watching them in the rain.

"We've got to stop bumping into each other like this?" Thea whispered mockingly as Mia walked up to her.

"Shut up," Mia whispered hastily back.

A young girl with long wavy light brown hair poked her head out of the doorway to the café to see if it was safe to come out yet. Mia recognized her as the girl they saw at the mall about a week ago, only this time instead of pigtails, her hair hung down in luxurious waves with her bangs pulled back by a white headband.

"Oh, hey, it's you two again!" she said as she spotted them and made her way down the steps.

"You know them?" Elliott asked in awe.

"Kind of… They helped me out at the mall the other day when I tripped in the parking lot." Lucy giggled.

"If you call 'helping' us running over and you being completely fine, then sure." Thea chuckled.

Lucy smiled widely at her. "It's the thought that counts!"

"So… how is it you two know each other?" Thea said, not at all nonchalantly. Mia sent her a glare like daggers.

"Oh, she's my little sister," Elliott said nervously.

"Half sister," Lucy interjected. "And I can tell you, this moodiness he's got going on is definitely from his dad's side, because I've happily avoided all of…" She gestured to Elliott. "That."

"Way to overshare to strangers, Lu," he said, crossing his arms and blatantly avoiding eye contact with Mia and Thea. The blush growing across his cheeks didn't go unnoticed by Mia.

"Oh, they're not strangers!" she said, waving him off.

"Well, technically we never actually introduced ourselves, so… we kind of are?" Mia said, shrugging.

Lucy stared at her for a few seconds before her peppy demeanor returned.

"Well, that's easily fixed! I'm Lucy, and Mr. Pouty here is Elliott!"

"Would you stop calling me moody and pouty?" Elliott said, annoyed.

Thea leaned into Mia. "It's not like she's lying," she whispered to her, and they both chuckled.

Lucy laughed too, as if she heard the joke, and Elliott's face got even more red than before. He turned away from them out of embarrassment.

"I'm Mia. It's nice to meet you," she said, holding her hand out for Lucy to shake it.

"And I'm Thea!"

"Mia and Thea?" Lucy chuckled. "Well, that's easy to remember!"

"Yeah, the magic of randomized roommates," Mia said sarcastically.

"Anyway..." Thea said, leaning in towards Elliott. He jumped when he saw how close she had gotten to him. "Is there any reason you've been ghosting my girl Mia here, Elliott?"

Mia felt her heart drop into her stomach, and Elliott's face went ghostly pale. Thea had always been a straightforward person, but this was a complete one-eighty from their conversation.

"Thea!" she hissed at her.

"Whoa," Lucy said. "What's with the third degree all of the sudden? I thought we were all getting along?"

"Lucy, it's all right," Elliott said.

"No, it's not all right. She can't just come at you like that!" She turned from her brother back to Thea. "What's your problem, anyway?"

Lucy's demeanor completely changed at Thea grilling her brother, and Mia made a mental note not to get in between this family. She couldn't believe that such a peppy and upbeat girl like Lucy would have an anger problem.

"I didn't come at him. I just asked him a question. That's all.

No need to get so upset." Thea just shrugged nonchalantly, which seemed to make Lucy even angrier.

"Thea… just drop it," Mia begged, and Thea turned towards her.

"No, it's been bothering you for days now, and when you have a problem, then we both do." She crossed her arms and turned back towards Elliott. "So, tell me, Elliott, why have you been avoiding Mia?"

"I… um…" Elliott said, scratching the back of his head awkwardly.

"Wait… avoiding?" Lucy said, her eyes opening wide with some sort of revelation Mia didn't understand. A sly grin came over her face, and Mia wasn't sure what it meant, but she didn't like it.

"Yeah. Avoiding, that's kinda what ghosting means," Thea exclaimed, clearly annoyed that she hadn't gotten her answer yet.

Lucy looked between Mia and Elliott, and he gave his sister a pleading look.

"You've been avoiding this girl?" Lucy said, turning on her brother almost as fast as she changed moods before.

"I—no…"

"Don't lie to me, Elliott!" Lucy said, smacking her brother's arm.

"Ow!" he exclaimed, rubbing the spot she hit. "I wasn't lying. I—"

"How can you say that when Mia *saw* you look right at her and then turn around to run away from her?" Thea shouted.

"Guys…" Mia attempted to interject, but the three of them continued to shout over each other.

"You did *what*?" Lucy said, smacking Elliott again.

"Would you quit doing that? How am I supposed to explain myself if you don't even give me the chance to?" Elliott yelled, clearly at the end of his rope.

As they continued to argue, Mia was getting increasingly more overwhelmed. This wasn't even their battle to fight, and yet they were blowing it out of proportion. Leave it to Thea to start a fight that she had nothing to do with, and it seemed like Lucy was just as headstrong as she was.

She felt like all of this was pointless. Did she want to know why he was avoiding her? Yes, but she didn't want it this way. None of that mattered anymore.

"Guys!" Mia yelled at the top of her lungs.

All three of them quickly shut their mouths and stared at her.

"You need to stop all of this pointless arguing! It's clearly going nowhere, and this entire thing is stupid in the first place, so just... drop it, okay?" Mia pleaded.

"But—" Thea started.

"No 'buts'!" Mia snapped at her. "This isn't about you!" She turned and pointed at both her and Lucy. "It's not about you or Lucy, so you two just need to... shut up for the moment. Did he blatantly ghost me? Yes, that's pretty much been established."

Elliott looked away and rubbed the back of his head, ashamed.

"And maybe I'll never know why, but what really matters is that he's sorry and won't do it again. Right?" Mia said, turning towards Elliott. She felt like she was scolding a child, but that's just what she had to do at this moment.

Elliot just stared at her, astonished at her anger.

"Right?" she pressed again when he didn't immediately respond.

He blinked a few times, coming back to his senses.

"Y-yes. You're absolutely right," he said, looking her in the eyes for the first time since they started talking. "I really am so sorry for the discomfort I caused you. I didn't mean to. I was just... I don't know, it sounds dumb, but what happened when we first met was really embarrassing, and I guess I didn't want to face that again. It was stupid of me to do, and again, I'm really sorry."

Mia took that in, feeling like it wasn't the entire story. But he gave her what she wanted to hear, so she couldn't be angry at him for that. She was still frustrated at this entire situation and how Thea had instigated and dealt with it.

"Thank you for apologizing," she said and turned back towards Thea. "I'm done here, so either you can continue being petty with your new partner in crime, or you can come inside with me." She started walking back towards the café and stopped next to Elliott. She spoke without making eye contact, and any emotion she had shown before was now gone. "It was nice meeting you. I'll see you around campus... I guess."

She stepped into the café, leaving the three of them standing in the rain.

Chapter Ten

"Lucy, I can tell you want to shout at me right now, so just quit it with the silent treatment and say what you want to say," Elliott said.

He was driving her home after their trip to the café. A "brother-sister catch-up," as she called it, but she hadn't said a thing to him since they said goodbye to Thea.

When she didn't respond after a few minutes, he pulled the car over and parked on the side of the road.

"What are you doing?" Lucy asked, confused and annoyed at the same time.

"Oh, so you can speak! I thought you'd lost your voice after all of that shouting you'd done," he said sarcastically.

She gave him a dirty look but once again turned back towards the window, giving him the silent treatment.

"I'm not moving this car until you say what you've gotta say to me. I know you didn't get it all out during that shit show of a fight. Thanks for that embarrassment, by the way."

She rolled her eyes at him, knowing he could see her in the

window's reflection. She prepared to stay silent for however long it took before Elliott gave up on her.

"Lucy, you're acting like a child. Just say something already!" he shouted, and she jumped in response. He never raised his voice at her like that.

"What?" She spun on him. "What would you like me to say? Hm? That I should be supportive of your actions to ignore this poor girl?"

"No, I already knew you weren't supportive of my plan to avoid her."

"Yeah, avoiding and blatantly showing you're ignoring her are two very different things, Elliott! She said she saw you doing it! Don't you even feel bad?"

"Of course I feel bad, Lucy!" He slammed his hands on the steering wheel. "Every second I had to do that felt like torture, and hearing how hurt she was to know I was doing it? It makes me feel sick." He sat back in his seat and ran his hand down his face.

"But you're still going to treat her like she's nothing to you?" she asked sadly.

"I-I don't want to. You have to know that, Lucy," he pleaded, turning towards her. "But I can't risk my dad finding out and hurting her somehow…"

"You don't know for sure he would do something like that."

"We can have this conversation a million times, Lucy, but you know, I know for damned sure he caused Ava's death."

She turned back towards the windshield and stared out towards the road in front of them, thinking. There was no use arguing in what they both knew was the truth.

"Could you not just… be friends with her, at least?" she asked, eyes unmoving from the road.

"Friendship leads to relationships, which leads to my father's interference, which could lead to her death," he stated coldly.

"You're so paranoid." She turned towards him and crossed her arms.

"Better paranoid than someone hurt."

"Oh, come on, Elliott! Just give it a chance!" She threw her arms up and shifted in her seat to face him better. "If you're so worried, we can have someone keep watch on her. Even Zeke could take a round on full moons if you're that concerned!"

He hadn't even considered having others to help keep her safe. It seemed ridiculous that he hadn't thought about that before now, but he felt it had to be him and him alone who kept her safe, which, of course, shouldn't be the case. It was just another stupid wolf instinct from the soulmate bond he didn't ask for.

"E?" Lucy said after he hadn't spoken in a while.

"Sorry... I just—I don't know why I never really thought of that as an option before."

"Seriously? What, you thought you had to be the macho 'protector'?" She laughed at him. "You're so dumb sometimes."

"This coming from the girl who didn't know what ghosting meant," he teased back.

"It's not that I didn't know what it meant. It's that ghosting is normally used for online stuff, not to ignore someone in real life."

"Pretty sure you can use them interchangeably."

"Yeah... you really can't... Hey, wait, don't change the subject!" She playfully punched him in the arm. "So, are you going to actually talk to Mia now, or are you still going to pretend she doesn't exist?"

"I suppose..." He sighed and rubbed his eyes. "I suppose I could try doing things your way." Lucy's face lit up with a smile. "But if I sense one thing wrong, it's stopping immediately."

"Once again, you're paranoid." She crossed her arms. "Nothing's going to happen."

"I'm just cautious," he said, turning the car back on. "Unlike you, who throws caution to the wind every chance she gets."

"Eh, life's just more fun that way." She leaned back in the seat with her arms behind her head, finally satisfied to be getting things her way.

"Yeah, till it gets you in trouble." He smiled at her

overconfidence.

"It hasn't yet!" She laughed. A smug look was painted on her face, and Elliott couldn't help but scoff at her.

"Whatever. Let's just get you home."

He pulled out onto the road, and they continued their drive back to his mother's house.

"So, I guess going out was a total bust for helping you figure stuff out," Thea said jokingly as she took a seat at the table Mia chose in the café. Beads of water from the rain were still stuck in her hair, and they sparkled in the lights that hung from the ceiling.

The shop itself wasn't very big, but it was a quaint place with a rustic theme. Usually there were plenty of people here trying to get breakfast, but because of the rain, there were only about three other groups in the building.

It had been five whole minutes since Mia left the group outside, and she wondered what they could have been talking about for so long. She had chosen a seat near the window so she could watch them, but it seemed to be mostly Thea and Lucy ganging up on Elliott. She felt bad for him and thought about going back out to grab Thea by the sleeve of her track jacket and drag her inside, but that would've defeated the purpose of her dramatic exit.

"I do *not* want to talk about it, Thea," Mia said, keeping her eyes glued to the menu in her hands. It annoyed her that Thea would bring that up so nonchalantly after everything that had just happened.

Thea definitely caught the angst in her tone. But it wasn't like she didn't deserve it.

"Wow, okay. There's no need to be rude just because things didn't go super great out there," she said as she shook the water out of her hair.

"Super great?" she asked, slamming the menu down on the table. "Thea, it was like you two were out for blood! It was uncalled for and childish! And I have every right to be upset with you. I didn't ask for you to go after him like that. I didn't need you to 'help me out' in any way. If I was interested in finding out what was going on, I could've done it myself." She crossed her arms and sank down in her chair, looking away from Thea.

"I was just trying to be a good friend, but if that's how you feel, then fine," she said, picking up her menu to cut off their eye contact.

Mia sighed. Thea could be difficult to deal with sometimes, but things would just continue to be awkward between them if she didn't fix it. She couldn't blame her for trying to help if her heart was in the right place, even if everything got out of control.

Mia sat back up in her chair and took a deep breath.

"Look, I know you had good intentions, Thea, but maybe next time you could just... take a second to think about the repercussions before acting on your first instinct?"

Thea continued to stay silent and examine the menu. Was she really playing this game when Mia was trying to settle things between them? She knew she was stubborn, but this was a bit much.

"Thea? Are you gonna say anything, or just continue to let this sit awkwardly between us?"

Thea huffed, obviously upset that she knew Mia was right. "Fine." She set the menu down on the table but still didn't look Mia in the eyes. "I guess... I did act a little..." She waved her hand in the air, trying to come up with the correct word to use. "Rashly?"

"And?"

"And... I'm sorry, okay?" she admitted with a scowl on her face. "It won't happen again."

"Thanks, Thea." Mia couldn't help but crack a sly grin at how hard it was for Thea to admit she was wrong.

"What are you suddenly so chipper about?"

"That was really hard for you to get out, wasn't it?" She chuckled.

"It was, actually!" she joked, crumpling up a napkin and throwing it at Mia.

"Excuse me, are you two ready to order?" a small blonde waitress said, interrupting their giggling.

"Oh yeah, sorry," Thea said. "I'll have the turkey club with a side of fries, please."

"Got it, and for you?"

"And I'll just have a bowl of chicken noodle soup, please," Mia ordered.

"No problem. I'll get those out as soon as I can," the waitress said as she took their menus and walked away.

As soon as she was out of earshot, Thea leaned in to gossip.

"So, not to bring up the whole Elliott thing again, but…"

Mia raised her eyebrow at her, wondering where this was going.

"What are you gonna do if you see him again?"

"I dunno, either talk with him if he wants to talk, or ignore each other if that's what he wants. I don't really think I care all that much anymore." She shrugged.

Though the thought of never talking to him again made her stomach drop. She couldn't understand it, but she wanted to know him better.

"You really think he'd ignore you still after all of that?"

"Probably not, but I also really don't want to deal with the way I scolded him like a child." Mia laughed nervously, getting embarrassed just thinking about how she flipped out on everyone.

"Well, I don't think he'll be ignoring you anymore, not with the way he was looking at you." She raised her eyebrows suggestively at Mia.

"Oh no, I am definitely not interested in that," Mia said, putting her hands up defensively.

"I don't know, Mia… The way you were blushing at him…"

she teased.

"Oh, shut up!" Mia threw back the napkin that Thea had thrown at her earlier.

"Well, I hope you see him again. You could use a few more friends around here."

"Don't tell me you're sick of hanging with me all the time," Mia said sarcastically.

"Nah, it's not that. You just don't get out a lot unless it's with me, so maybe someone else can finally drag you out of that dorm room."

"I only stay in our room so much because it's quiet, and online game nights with Erika and Peter are easier in a secluded room than out in the campus center."

"You do online game nights? Since when?"

"I schedule them during your club meetings so you don't have to listen to all the 'nerd talk.'"

"Wow. And you never thought to invite me," Thea said with sarcasm.

"You don't even like MMOs. Why would you care?"

"It's like you've got this whole other secret life I don't even know about," she said dramatically, teasing Mia for thinking hanging out online with her high school friends was more exciting than going out with her.

"Well, would you like to join next time? We're looking for a fourth player to round out our team."

"Nah, I'm good. But hey, you could always ask Elliott." She sang his name, and Mia groaned.

She was about to object to Thea's suggestion when their food arrived.

"We are so not done talking about this!" Thea said as they dug into their lunch.

CHAPTER ELEVEN

IT WAS FINALLY MONDAY, and Elliott strode through campus with as much confidence as he could muster, just hoping he might run into Mia somewhere. It seemed silly to him, being excited about running into her again and talking to her for real, especially after their entire interaction on Saturday.

He'd had crushes before, but they never made him nervous to interact with the person. He didn't know how to deal with this kind of situation at all, and that was more than a little terrifying.

He was meandering through the campus center when he spotted her, and his heart had to have skipped a few beats.

She was sitting at a table near the juice bar, her laptop open as she typed away. Her hair was down for once, pulled back away from her face with a black headband, and the way the sun hit her made the blue tint stand out even more than usual. She looked like she was concentrating super hard on whatever she was working on. He wondered if he should bother her, but after a moment of thought, he decided this might be his only chance.

He took a deep breath and attempted to shake out his nerves.

"You've got this," he whispered to himself, not that it helped him in the least.

He walked up to her, attempting to control his breathing.

As he got closer, he noticed her laptop was covered in stickers of various comic characters, some of which were his favorites too. It was nice to know they were into some of the same things. Maybe this wouldn't be so hard after all...

"Uh, hey, Mia," he said, stopping in front of her. She didn't look up at him or acknowledge him at all. Was she ignoring him now as payback? He wouldn't blame her if she did, but it still hurt a bit. "Mia?" he tried again.

"Come on, come on, come on," she whispered to herself as she clicked her mouse and pressed harder on her keyboard.

It only now occurred to him she might not be working on homework at all. He moved a bit to the side of her and saw she was actually playing a video game, and not one that he recognized either.

"Yes!" she hissed as she won whatever game it was and finally looked away from her laptop. She let out a small squeak of fright when she noticed he was standing there watching her play.

"Oh, I'm sorry. I didn't mean to scare you!" he said hastily.

She took out the wireless earbuds he hadn't seen earlier. "N-no, it's fine. I'm sorry, I didn't see you there."

"I, uh, saw you as I was passing through and just wanted to come over to say I was sorry about how everything went down on Saturday."

"Oh. I uh... I think I'm kind of the one that needs to apologize." She looked down nervously, unable to meet his gaze. "I shouldn't have talked to you like that, and Thea never would've even started that argument if I didn't tell her about... well, you know." She looked at him and then quickly averted her eyes, clearly embarrassed about bringing up how he ignored her.

"Technically, none of this would've happened if I didn't ignore you in the first place, so..."

They stayed quiet, avoiding eye contact for a while, unsure of what to say to each other.

"Well, we can sit here and play the blame game all day, but I should probably get to class," Mia said, packing up her laptop.

"Oh yeah, of course." He looked around a bit before thinking of how he could continue talking to her, unable to let her go just yet. "So, what was that game you were playing, anyway?"

She started walking toward the classrooms in the campus center, and he followed her.

"Oh, it's just an MMO called Duel of Ages. You pretty much just fight on a team to defend your castle from other players. My friends from high school and I got really into it over the summer, so now we hop on and play whenever we can."

"Sounds fun. I'm usually pretty bad at games like that."

"Aw, it just takes a little practice. I hate playing with anyone but my friends 'cause people can be pretty rude on games like that if they don't win."

"Hm, that sounds annoying."

"Yeah, it is."

They walked in silence for a moment, and Mia looked like she was contemplating something.

"Though, if you wanted to try playing sometime, I'm sure my friends wouldn't mind an extra player on our team," she finally said. "We could definitely show you how. We're kind of lacking a good healer at the moment."

"Oh, yeah, definitely. I'd be down for that," he said, just a bit too enthusiastically.

Mia smiled at him, and god was it a pretty smile. He felt his heart melt a little in that moment and had to remind himself he was just going to keep this as a friendship relationship.

"If you wanna swap numbers, I can text you when our next game is gonna be," she said.

"Sure, that sounds good to me," he said, smiling eagerly at her.

He took out his phone and opened it up to the contacts, as she did the same. They swapped phones to put their numbers in and then handed them back.

They continued to walk down the hallway before Mia suddenly stopped, and Elliott almost ran into her. She turned towards him, and he realized it was because this was where her class was.

"Well, this is my stop," she said.

"Oh! It was, uh, nice chatting with you," he responded nervously.

"You too. I'll text you those details later!"

"Looking forward to it!"

She walked inside, and he wished their conversation wasn't over so soon.

"So, that's her, huh?"

Elliott spun around to see Zeke lounging up against the wall behind him. He had one leg up supporting him, with his hands in his pockets. He looked like a typical bad boy standing there, and Elliott couldn't help but notice all the girls that stared at him as they walked by.

"She's definitely pretty, I'll give you that. But with that nerdy appeal she's got going on, I'd definitely say she's not my type," Zeke continued. "She does look kinda familiar, though…" He scratched his head, trying to remember.

"Well, it doesn't really matter if she's 'your type' now, does it?" Elliott said, walking away from the classroom and back towards the exit, resisting the urge to growl at his friend for his unnecessary comment. "And what are you doing here, anyway? Were you just following me this whole time?"

"From a distance!" he said as he jogged to catch up to Elliott. "And don't you worry; I didn't hear any part of your conversation. I gave you two lovebirds complete and total privacy."

"First of all, we're not lovebirds. Second, there was nothing to overhear, anyway. We were talking about video games. And third, if you weren't here to eavesdrop and spy on me, why are you here?"

"Well, how am I supposed to be a crucial part of this 'keep her safe' plan, if I don't even know what she looks like?" He casually put his arms behind his head as he walked.

"Oh, I don't know, Zeke, wait until you actually meet her like a normal person would?"

"Nah, knowing you, that'd take too long to happen. And the next full moon is way too close for me to wait around for you to make your move."

"Make my move? Zeke, I am just staying friends with her!" he said, exasperated.

"For now," Zeke said, pointing his finger at Elliott and raising his eyebrows.

"Whatever, dude, it's not happening," Elliott said, pushing the doors of the campus center open to start his walk from the quad to his car.

Zeke rushed out after him.

"Besides, there's probably no way of her liking me back like that after I avoided her the way I did. I'm surprised she's even willing to give me the time of day," he said sadly.

"Oh, you're being too hard on yourself, dude. You're a super nice guy once you get past your brooding, not to mention attractive. She'd be dumb not to like you."

Elliott stopped walking and raised his eyebrow at Zeke. "Did you just call me attractive?"

"Hey, man, I just tell it like it is. I've lived long enough to tell when someone's attractive or not. Don't make it weird."

"Yeah, you kind of already did."

They continued walking in silence and made it all the way to the parking lot before Zeke spoke again.

"Y'know, your sister and I have a bet going now."

Elliott stopped walking and turned towards Zeke in surprise.

"You and my sister? You don't even like Lucy."

"That's beside the point." He waved him off. "We have a bet going about how long it's going to take for you two to finally get together."

Elliott groaned and rolled his eyes as he continued walking, ready to be done with this conversation. Zeke, however, caught up with him and continued talking anyway.

"She thinks you'll be together by Christmas, but I give it till Halloween. So don't let me down, buddy," he said, patting Elliott on the back.

"You two are insufferable." He groaned.

"Wouldn't be your best friend if I wasn't!"

CHAPTER TWELVE

MIA AND THEA ROAMED through the quad, looking for a nice patch of grass to sit under some shade. It had been four days since her encounter with Elliott, and she had been unusually excited to see him again.

"Oh, there's a spot!" Thea shouted, interrupting her thoughts and dashing away from Mia. Her big canvas and easel bounced awkwardly under her arm as she ran.

It wasn't a particularly special spot, just a giant tree in the middle of the park-like space of the quad. Perfect for hanging out in between classes since the academic buildings surrounded the area.

Thea made it to the spot she had picked out and set up her painting station underneath the tree before Mia had even meandered her way over.

"So, tell me again why exactly I needed to come out here with you?" Mia said as she approached her.

"Because my assignment is to paint a real-life scene with movement to it. So the quad is the best place to do that!"

"Still doesn't explain why I had to come along."

"Because I needed someone to keep me company, of course!" she said as she sketched out the outline for her painting.

"Of course," Mia said sarcastically, pulling her phone out of the pocket of her jeans.

She was supposed to meet up with Elliott to show him the basics of Duel of Ages before they played a real game with Erika and Peter on Friday, but thanks to Thea that was going to have to take place outside, instead of in the lobby lounge of her dorm. She just hoped the Wi-Fi around campus worked as well as the ones in the dorms did; otherwise, it was going to be a bit of a struggle.

She sent Elliott a quick text telling him where to meet her.

"What, do you have something better to be doing?"

"No… not at the moment," Mia said, sitting down in front of the tree and leaning against it.

"Not at the moment," Thea repeated, tapping her paintbrush on her chin before pointing it at Mia. "Kinda sounds like you do, though."

"Hey, why are you focusing on me when you should be painting?" she shot back.

Thea scowled at her before returning to her project.

It wasn't long before Elliott arrived, but he wasn't alone. Why would he bring a friend along when she was just showing him how to play a video game? But the boy with him looked strangely familiar…

She was trying to decipher where she'd seen the boy with the black faux hawk before when Elliott yelled to her.

"Hey Mia!" he shouted from across the quad.

Thea looked at him, and then back at Mia, confused.

"What is he doing here?" she whispered, while he was still out of earshot.

Thea still wasn't quite over the argument she had on Saturday. Mia was pretty sure she was just too embarrassed about what happened, and she wasn't actually mad at him at all.

She gave Elliott a wave before answering Thea.

"I'm teaching him how to play Duel of Ages for my game night on Friday," she said, standing up and wiping the dirt off of her pants.

"Your what?"

"The MMO I told you about on Saturday?"

"I only vaguely remember that conversation," she said stubbornly, looking back at her painting.

"Well, it was your idea for me to invite him, so you can't be mad at me," she said, placing her hands on her hips.

"Well, then... why didn't you tell me?"

"Because you pulled me out here with you."

"Well, I wouldn't have done that if I'd known!"

"Oh, hey, Thea, I didn't know you were gonna be here too!" Elliott said, giving her a smile.

"Likewise," she said back, her eyes flicking to him before immediately going back to her painting.

"Okay..." Mia said awkwardly before walking over to Elliott. "Well, I figured we could just set up at that picnic table over there so we're not lying in the grass the whole time."

"Sounds good to me." He stood there smiling at her again, his blue eyes sparkling in the sun. She smiled back before reminding herself not to get attached to him. They were there to play a video game and nothing more.

Elliott's friend cleared his throat to remind him he was still there, which he had clearly forgotten about in the two minutes they had been talking.

"Oh, right! Mia, this is Zeke. Zeke, this is Mia," he said, moving away so Zeke could get by.

"Nice to meet you," Zeke said, offering his hand.

She looked at his hand, and then back up to his face. He seemed like a nice person, but some part of her was screaming for her to run away. She slowly took his hand and flinched at how cold it was.

"Sorry, poor circulation." He shrugged.

She nodded in response and gave him an awkward grin, not sure what to make of him.

"Sorry, he just insisted on coming with me and wouldn't take no for an answer," Elliott said nervously.

"Oh, that's all right. I don't mind the extra company," Mia said, even if a little part of it was a lie.

"If there's ever a chance to see Elliott get his ass beat by a girl at a video game, then you can bet I'm gonna be there to—" Zeke froze when he turned his head towards Thea.

"Uh, Zeke, you okay there, dude?" Elliott asked.

Mia could practically see the gears turning in Zeke's head as he tried to figure something out. He suddenly let out a gasp and pointed at Thea.

"That's where I know you from!" he exclaimed.

Thea turned to look at him, and recognition immediately crossed her face.

"See, I knew you looked familiar. You two were at that frat party a couple of weeks ago, weren't you?" Zeke asked enthusiastically.

"Uh…" Thea said, looking at Mia. Neither of them knew what to say as they stared at each other and him.

"I only saw you for a split second," he said, pointing at Mia. "When you came and dragged her out of the party while we were having such a good time dancing."

It suddenly hit Mia at once when he said that. She couldn't believe she hadn't recognized him sooner. She had been watching him dance with Thea all night. Though mostly it was just the back of his head, the pleather jacket should have been a dead giveaway.

"Okay, there is no way you two just happen to be friends," Thea said. "Between running into your sister at the mall, and now this? That can't be a coincidence."

Zeke simply shrugged. "It's a small town."

"Says the one who hasn't lived here his whole life," Elliott rebutted.

"I am curious, though…" Zeke started. "Why did you two run

away like that?"

"I don't see why that's any of your business," Thea spat.

"Well, you did leave me standing there rather awkwardly. I think I'm within my right to ask for an explanation."

"Was that not the party you beat someone up at?" Elliott chimed in.

"Wait a minute. You're the one that punched Jared in the face?" Thea exclaimed.

Mia felt her cheeks heat at the mention of what had happened at the party. She did not want to relive that moment again, and she especially didn't want Elliott to know about it.

"Is that the name of that redheaded guy? He was just being a sleaze to a bunch of chicks that night, and guys like that need to be taught a lesson," he said nonchalantly.

"Wow, what a gentleman you are," Thea said sarcastically, rolling her eyes.

"Wait a minute; is that why you ran out? Did he try to pull a fast one on you?" he retorted, looking directly at Mia.

"I'd… I'd rather not talk about it," Mia said, looking away from him.

"Seriously, if he hurt you—" Zeke said, taking a step towards her.

Thea opened her mouth to yell at him, but Elliott beat her to the punch.

"Just drop it, Zeke," he said sternly, looking like he was fighting the urge to scream. "If she doesn't want to talk about it, she doesn't have to."

Mia looked at the two of them, her heartbeat pounding in her chest as they seemed to exchange a silent conversation. She looked over at Thea, who simply shrugged at her.

Zeke put his hands up defensively. "All right, message received. Sorry, Mia."

"It's fine," she said quietly before taking a deep breath. "How about we get to it, then?" She tried her best to change the subject and gestured for them to move over to the picnic table.

"Right, sounds good to me. Come on, Zeke," Elliott said.

They started to make their way towards the nearby picnic table, but Zeke didn't follow.

"Actually, I think I'll stick around here with... I'm sorry, did I catch your name?" Zeke asked, turning to Thea.

"You didn't," she said emotionlessly.

"Come on, man, don't bother her," Elliott pleaded. "Hey, what happened to watching me get my butt kicked?"

"Oh, but this just seems way more interesting," Zeke teased.

"Dude, don't be an asshole," Elliott said.

"It's fine," Thea finally said, keeping her eyes on her painting. "If he wants to stay, then let him stay."

"You sure?" Mia asked, concerned.

"Yeah, sure." She turned to look at Mia, refusing to make eye contact with either of the boys. "I know how to tune people out pretty well, so it's no big deal." She shrugged.

Zeke made a hissing noise. "Harsh."

"Well... all right, if you say so," Mia said. "We'll just be over there if you need us."

Thea gave them a thumbs-up as she turned back towards her painting, attempting to hyper-focus so she wouldn't have to hear Zeke prattling on about whatever he felt like.

Mia and Elliott made their way over to the table and quietly started setting up their laptops.

"So..." Mia started, breaking the silence. "If Zeke was at that party, were you there with him, or does he not drag you out to things like that, like Thea does to me?"

"Uh... no, I wasn't there. I, um..." He paused, thinking of what she didn't know. "I haven't really been a party person since, um... recently, I guess."

Mia wanted to ask more about that vague answer but felt she shouldn't be prying into his personal life. Not when she barely even knew him.

"Um, all right. Why don't we get to the game then?" she finally said.

They both logged on and she showed him the basics of playing, and he was right; video games were definitely not his thing. But playing with him on their team would be a better option than someone random like they usually did, and he'd get better with time.

Every so often, she would have to lean over towards his computer to show him how to do something. Being so close to him made her heart hammer in her chest, and despite how many times she pushed those strange feelings for him down, they kept coming right back up.

She was not normally a nervous person around strangers, not that she could quite consider him a stranger at this point, but for some reason being around him just made her feel weird. She had assumed at first that it might be a crush, but whatever this was felt different from that, almost as if an invisible force was pulling her towards him. She did not like it at all.

She just wished she could be as calm as he was with their proximity to each other. Anytime she leaned in towards him, he continued to stay cool and collected, his breathing steady, while her voice would constantly stutter.

Before she knew it, an entire two hours had passed, and Elliott had vastly improved his game. He wasn't dying nearly as much, and despite her awkwardness of being close to him, she was actually having a great time.

"I think we should call it a day," Mia said after their last game.

"So whaddaya think, am I up to the challenge of playing with you and your friends tomorrow night?" he said with a goofy, lopsided grin.

"I'd say you're gonna do just fine." She chuckled.

"Thank you so much for inviting me to play with you guys, and even taking the time to teach me the basics. I know I'm not the best, but it still means a lot."

"Hey, it's better than using a stranger as our fourth." She shrugged. "To be honest, I was getting annoyed with doing that every time we played, and I really don't mind showing you how everything works."

"Well, thank you anyway." He laughed. "We should probably go save Thea from Zeke now."

"Yeah, you're probably right."

Looking over at them, they were both sitting in the grass, and Thea was actually laughing as the two of them talked. Mia couldn't tell if she had finished her project or if she just abandoned it altogether.

Just two hours ago, she was acting like she didn't want to be around him at all, and now they were laughing? Thea wasn't one to get over a grudge so easily. What could've changed so fast?

Elliott had the same look of confusion on his face as Mia did, and they quickly packed up and walked back over to Zeke and Thea.

"Well, you two certainly look a lot more friendly than when we left you," Mia commented as she walked up to them.

"You two were gone for a while. We had to do something to curb the boredom once she was done ignoring me," Zeke said.

"Oh yeah? And how long did it take for her to stop ignoring you?" Mia asked.

"About…" He paused for dramatic effect and looked at his wrist as if he was wearing a watch. "One hour and twenty-three minutes," Zeke said.

"You timed it?" Thea laughed, smacking him on the arm.

"I was intrigued by how long you said you could go, so, yeah. I did."

"Did you finish your painting at least?" Mia asked.

"Oh yeah, I did!" Thea got up and turned the easel so they could see it. "Still not sure how I feel about it, though."

It looked just like the campus, but instead of people walking by, it looked like they were practically dancing across the canvas. Mia saw a lot of the art that Thea made, but it was never less impressive when she made a new painting.

"Oh, wow, that looks fantastic!" Elliott said.

"Thanks. I've definitely done better, though." She brushed off the compliment, as she always seemed to do when someone liked her art.

"Oh, just shut up and take the compliment," Mia said.

Thea rolled her eyes, chuckling, and Zeke finally stood up.

"Well, it's about time we get going, I think," Zeke said.

"Yeah, you're right. I'll see you online tomorrow night, I guess," Elliott said, suddenly sounding way more nervous than he had in the last two hours.

"Eight o'clock, and don't be late or we will start without you!" Mia said sternly. "Erika's really impatient, so she won't let us wait."

"Got it," he said, giving her a thumbs-up. "And I'll see you around too, Thea!"

She gave him a quick wave as she picked up her things so they could go back inside, but as soon as she saw they were out of earshot, she rushed over to Mia.

"So?" she sang in Mia's ear.

"So... what?" Mia asked, confused.

"So, how was it? Are you two getting comfortable with each other? Did he ask you out on a real date? Come on, give me all the details!" She rattled off question after question as she shook Mia's arm.

"Details? Thea, I was just showing him how to play a video game. It wasn't a date."

"Oh, come on! That was totally a date!" she said, hopping up and down like a child.

"Nope. Just friends. A guy and a girl can be just friends without it getting romantic, you know." She crossed her arms and leaned back on the tree.

"I know that! But you two are so cute together; even Zeke thinks so!"

She looked back at Elliott and Zeke in the distance and saw Zeke quickly turn away from her gaze and laugh as Elliott's face turned red. Was Zeke teasing him as well?

She quickly regained her focus and turned back towards Thea.

"Zeke? What, is he your best friend now? You ignore him for over an hour and a half and then talk for half an hour and suddenly you're all buddy-buddy?"

"No! He just—it's actually kind of funny, really." She scratched the back of her head nervously. "He and Lucy have a bet going on with how long it'll take you two to get together."

"Excuse me?" Mia said, surprised.

"Yeah, Lucy says before Christmas, so Zeke said before Halloween. I, of course, took the middle ground holiday and said you'd be together by Thanksgiving because I know you. It's gonna take you a while to even feel like you'd want to date him and—"

"You went in on the bet?" Mia yelled, pushing herself off the tree, angry that Thea would bet on her love life.

"Of course! What kind of best friend would I be if I didn't?" she said jokingly.

"A good one?"

"Oh, shut up, you don't really mean that!" She giggled.

"I know it's not a huge deal to you, Thea, but it's not something I would expect my best friend to do," she said, crossing her arms and sighing. "I'm sure Elliott wouldn't be happy about it either. I'm guessing that's what you two were laughing about when we walked over?"

"Yeah..."

Mia rubbed her temples, feeling a headache forming.

"Anyway, try not to get with him until after Halloween, okay? I wanna win this one and stick it to Zeke," Thea said, with a fire in her eyes. The heat of competition was already getting to her head.

Mia just rolled her eyes and started walking back towards their dorm.

"Hey, wait! You're not gonna help me pack up?" Thea shouted.

"Nope! I *bet* you can do it all by yourself!" She waved back without looking at her.

"Ha. Ha. Very funny," she shouted sarcastically, but Mia just kept walking, ignoring her. "Mia! Come on!"

She left Thea there to pick up her things herself.

What was she thinking? A bet on how long it would take for her to get with Elliott? She barely even knew him. Why would she want to date him? Sure, he was cute, but she refused to get into a relationship with a boy just because she thought he was nice to look at.

She wanted to know him first, even if some strange part of her already felt a pull towards him. He made her nervous to be around, yet she also felt a weird emptiness when he wasn't there. She didn't like it at all. This entire situation just confused her.

He, however, seemed perfectly fine being around her, so what were the chances he even liked her like that? Though if Zeke and Lucy had both started this bet, surely his feelings were taken into consideration to begin with?

Mia rubbed her temples as she walked. Her head was spinning from overthinking. If she couldn't even understand her own feelings, how was she supposed to deal with others placing bets on them?

CHAPTER THIRTEEN

IT HAD TAKEN EVERY ounce of self-control Elliott had to stay calm while Mia was showing him how to play Duel of Ages. Every time she leaned in towards him, her scent surrounded him, and he wanted nothing more but to pull her close and never let her go. He could hear her heart pounding away in her chest with nervousness when she was close to him, and it hurt so much to just ignore it all.

He let out a frustrated groan and pounded his fist on his desk at the memory from yesterday. Why did this have to be so difficult?

Looking at the time on his phone, he saw it was almost eight already. He opened his laptop and logged on to the game, wary of Mia's warning about being late.

Not a minute later, a chat box appeared with a message from Mia inviting him to their server. He smiled, amazed at how fast she'd sent him the link. He liked to think that she was waiting for him excitedly to get on, but he knew better. She and her friends were probably already logged on and talking. She must have just seen his name pop up and clicked on it.

He opened the link she sent, and it automatically had him join their game server. There was a text and voice chat option available, and he clicked on the little headset icon to join their discussion.

"Oh, wow, looks like your friend actually beat Peter here," a voice rang through his speakers. It was light, with a hint of a Spanish accent to it.

"Hey, Elliott," Mia said.

He could practically hear the smile on her face, but he wished he could see it, too.

"Hey," he said back.

"Erika, this is Elliott, Elliott, Erika," Mia introduced them, despite them not being able to see each other.

"Nice to meet you," Erika said. "Are you ready to kick some ass tonight?"

"I, uh... I guess so." He chuckled nervously.

"He doesn't sound very confident, Mia!" Erika teased.

"Oh, he did just fine yesterday, so I'm sure today will be no different." He smiled at her compliment. "Don't let Erika psych you out, Elliott, she's just joking around."

His nerves immediately disappeared with her reassuring words. It was astounding the power she had over him with just her voice.

"I'm here!" another voice suddenly chimed in.

Elliott looked at the clock to see it had just changed to eight.

"Cutting it real close, Peter," Erika said, annoyed.

"Sorry, sorry, I was on the phone with Dani and I lost track of time," Peter said.

A private message suddenly pinged up on Elliott's screen. Looking at it, he saw it was from Mia.

Dani is Peter's girlfriend, it read.

He quickly sent back a thumbs-up emoji.

"Yeah, whatever, talk to her on your own time," Erika said. "Now introduce yourself to Mia's friend so we can get on with the game."

"Oh yeah, that's right! Finally, another guy in the group! My name's Peter. It's nice to meet you."

"Hey, I'm Elliott. It's nice to meet you too. Well, meet your voices anyway."

Peter let out a small chuckle.

"You've got a sense of humor on you! That's good if you wanna hang with our little group," Peter said.

"Okay, we all know each other now. Can we get to the game already?" Erika said impatiently.

"All right, Miss Bossy Pants, choose the map so we can play," Peter said.

Sorry about her, Mia messaged him.

Oh, it's fine. She kind of reminds me of Zeke, he messaged back.

Mia let out a small laugh at his comment. He loved hearing her laugh so much; it was like music to his ears, and he could listen to it all day long.

"What's so funny?" Erika asked.

The character selection screen suddenly booted up on his computer, and they all picked who they were going to play as.

"Nothing at all," Mia said mischievously.

A grin spread across his face as he heard her lie through her teeth at their secret conversation.

"Mhm. Sure," Erika said sarcastically.

The map finally loaded, and the conversation came to an end. All of them were too busy concentrating on winning the battle.

Elliott walked through the campus center Monday afternoon. He had hoped that he might run into Mia just walking around campus now that his classes were over. He desperately wished to see her again, but he didn't want to give her the wrong idea by asking her to hang out with him. They were supposed to just stay friends after all.

It felt like his insides were getting torn apart every time he thought about being with her and then having to ignore it. He had to keep reminding himself that it was to protect her in the end. He had a small sliver of hope that one day his father wouldn't be an issue anymore and he could finally be happy, but those were thoughts better left for his dreams.

Finally, he saw her. She was sitting in a booth by the café. The sunlight streaming down on her face made her look even more ethereal than he already thought her to be. She had a book laid out in front of her, but she looked like she was more lost in thought than reading.

He wondered what she could be thinking about that had her so distracted. If only they were close enough that he could ask her about it.

He imagined pulling her to his chest and stroking his fingers through her hair, telling her everything would be okay. Letting her know she could tell him anything she wanted, and he would listen.

He shook his head, pushing those thoughts aside. He couldn't let himself think like that. It was only a matter of time before he let those thoughts get the better of him, causing him to do something drastic. It was a dangerous slope to go down, thinking of her like that.

"Are you planning on actually going over there to talk to her, or were you just going to stand here staring at her all day?" Zeke said, causing Elliott to jump.

He had snuck up on him while he was daydreaming.

"Zeke!" Elliott said, annoyed. "What are you even doing here?"

"Eh, I just woke up and figured I'd come bother you. You know, see what you were up to." He put his arms behind his head and leaned back against the wall behind them.

"Well, I'm not up to anything. So you can leave now," Elliott said, crossing his arms defensively.

"Yeah, sure, looks like you're up to nothing to me," he teased. "Nothing but creepily staring at Mia."

Elliott scoffed and rolled his eyes.

"I wasn't staring on purpose. I was… thinking."

"Yeah, thinking about Mia!" he sang.

"Shut up!" Elliott shoved Zeke playfully in the side, and he caught himself as he fell from the wall, laughing.

"So I'm right then!"

"Whatever, man, just leave it alone," Elliott said, slowly meandering his way towards Mia's spot at the café.

"Nah, I don't think I will. Not till I've won that bet."

"Ugh, that stupid bet. You two are ridiculous!"

"You mean you three."

Elliott stopped walking and turned back towards Zeke.

"Three?" he asked, confused.

"Yeah, Thea's officially in on it."

"Really? When did she—"

"Oh, hey, Elliott!" Mia yelled.

Elliott spun around to see Mia waving at them. He looked back at Zeke, who was now wearing a shit-eating grin on his face.

"Oh, shut up," Elliott whispered to him before turning and walking toward Mia. "Hey, Mia, what's up?"

"Not much, just catching up on some reading before class. What about you guys?"

"Just got out of class, so I figured I'd take a little walk," Elliott said, smiling awkwardly.

"I was just here to annoy him," Zeke said, pointing at Elliott with his thumb.

"Hm," she hummed in response. "Well, you guys wanna join me?"

She gestured to the seat across from her.

"Yeah, sure!" He smiled at her as he sat down, and she smiled back.

Gosh, that smile could light up an entire room. He desperately wanted to pull her in and steal that smile with a kiss. He shoved the thought back down as fast as it came.

Friends. They were just friends.

"Nah, I think I'm just gonna go. It was easy to annoy him when he was alone, but there's no point in trying now. It was good seeing you again, Mia," Zeke said, patting Elliott on the back.

"Good to see you too, Zeke," she said, laughing at his childish actions.

He waved at them and ran off to who knows where. He didn't quite care, just happy that Zeke had left him to have some alone time with Mia.

"Sorry about him," Elliott said. "Sometimes it feels like I'm babysitting when he's around."

"Ah, best friends are just like that sometimes." She waved him off. "So, how did you feel about our game night last Friday? I hadn't really gotten the chance to ask you about it yet."

"Oh, I had fun! Though I've gotta admit, Erika scares me a bit." He chuckled.

She laughed, the sound intoxicating to him, and he couldn't help but sigh.

"She sure is a lot sometimes, but you get used to her after a while." She paused, cocking her head to the side. "You do still want to play with us, right? She hasn't scared you off for real?"

"Oh, no, of course she hasn't!" He put his hands up defensively. "It's a fun thing to look forward to at the end of the week now."

"Well, I'm glad to hear that!" She smiled at him again, and his mind quickly raced back to thoughts of kissing her.

Her phone suddenly started beeping, drawing them out of each other's gaze. She looked down at it and frowned.

"Sorry, I set that so I wouldn't miss class," she said sadly.

She packed the book away in her bag and stood up. He followed her lead and got up from the table.

"I guess I'll be seeing you around then?" he asked.

"Yeah, definitely. It was good catching up, though!"

She waved at him and walked down the hall towards the classrooms.

He watched her as she walked away, wishing she didn't have to go. She turned around and gave him one last glance before continuing her trek to class. He wondered if that meant she was falling for him, too?

He took in a deep breath and repeated the mantra he'd had going in his head for days now.

They were friends. They had to just stay friends.

CHAPTER FOURTEEN

It was nearing the middle of October, and Elliott couldn't help but feel antsy. He caught his father's scent a few times recently, and it made him nervous to know he was around. He had yet to actually see him, and he wasn't sure if that was a good thing or something he should be wary about.

To make matters worse, he still had no idea if Mia felt the same about him as he did her, and it was driving him crazy. Lucy was right, of course. He wanted something more than friendship from this relationship. He tried so hard to resist the feelings, to shove them down as far as possible, but the more time he spent with her, the harder it was to do just that.

Elliott walked into the living room of their tiny apartment to see Zeke lying on their old sunken-in brown couch, watching some strange reality show.

"Dude, it's getting dangerously close to Halloween, so I'm gonna need you to ask Mia out already because I am not prepared to lose this bet to both Thea and your sister," he said without looking away from the TV.

Elliott still wasn't amused that those three had a bet going about when he'd ask Mia out, but he couldn't say he was surprised it happened. He still wasn't sure why Zeke had told him about it in the first place. Maybe it was to get a leg up on Lucy? He was, however, interested to hear that Thea was also involved in the bet now.

Maybe that meant Mia felt the same way he did? He wasn't sure where she'd placed her wager, so for all he knew, it was that they'd never be a couple. Not that any of that mattered when they couldn't be together anyway.

"You know why I can't do that, Zeke," he said, leaning on the wall between the living room and the hallway towards their bedrooms.

"Yeah, yeah, your dad or whatever." He waved his hand dramatically in the air before sitting up and looking at Elliott. "That was your excuse before, and look where you're at now. No interference from your dad. We haven't even seen him since we got here. He probably doesn't even know you came back."

"Trust me when I say he definitely knows I'm here. Just because you don't see him doesn't mean he's not around."

"I'm just saying, being friends with her is fine and all, but we've heard nothing for a month, so I think it's about time to take that next step."

"I'm fine with just being friends with her." Elliott shrugged, looking away from Zeke. They both knew that was a lie, but he hoped the more he told himself that, the more he'd believe it.

"Oh, who are you kidding?" Zeke said, getting up off the couch, suddenly full of concern. "I can hear your heart racing all the way out here every time you play that stupid game with her! All it takes is the sound of her voice! Dude, you've fallen hard, and I'm gonna need you to finally admit that to yourself."

"What happened to no super hearing in the apartment?"

"It's not like I can turn it on and off. My hearing works the same as yours. It's not any different just because I'm a vampire." He crossed his arms and shifted his weight.

"Well, you still shouldn't have been listening," Elliott said defensively.

"I already said I can't help it! And if you can't get it together by your next game night, I swear I'm gonna ask her out for you."

"Wouldn't that disqualify you from your little bet?" Elliott teased.

Zeke sneered at him. "Oh, shut it with your logic." He turned around and sat back down on the couch.

Elliott walked into their kitchen and grabbed a water bottle from the fridge. He was headed back down the hallway to his room when Zeke spoke again.

"In all seriousness, though... you've got to stop torturing yourself and just ask her out already."

"Zeke—"

"It's killing you to not be with her; I can tell. I've seen this kind of thing hundreds of times. Even felt it myself once before. Just ask her or you're gonna regret it forever," he said, looking away remorsefully.

He turned the TV off and got up, making his way to his room. He gave Elliott a supportive pat on the shoulder and a sad look as he walked past.

Then it was just Elliott, left alone in the hallway with his thoughts.

Maybe Zeke was right. Maybe nothing would happen to her after all. Maybe Elliott was just paranoid... But what if he wasn't?

He desperately wished that Tristan was around. His brother was the only one who could relate to this situation. But maybe if he was still in the area, he could find him himself.

"I'm going out for a bit!" he yelled to Zeke.

"Have fun, don't get caught!" he yelled back.

Elliott grabbed his keys and ran out the door.

Elliott hid his clothes in the same hollow tree trunk he had since he was eleven, in preparation to turn.

Hopefully Tristan was still close enough that he could just catch his scent to find him, though Elliott knew that if he were in his brother's position, he wouldn't have stuck around. He hadn't seen him on the last full moon, so why would he suddenly be here now?

He shook his limbs to loosen out his joints and jumped forward, immediately shifting to become a giant black wolf. He stretched out his legs and back, trying to release that dull ache that always came from the change.

He lifted his nose in the air and sniffed around, looking for anything familiar. After about a minute, he caught something. His brother's smell. It was faint, but it being there meant he couldn't have gotten far.

He took off in a sprint, following the scent to the best of his ability. He sped through the winding trees like a bullet, following the scent towards the college campus. What was his brother doing all the way out here?

Then he saw him, just on the edge of the woods. His brown fur blended in with the surrounding darkness. He was much bigger than Elliott was, and yet he still almost missed him.

He reached out to his brother's mind. "Tristan!" he said, running over.

His brother didn't move a muscle, concentrating on something Elliott couldn't see.

"Tristan?" he tried again, hoping his brother's change to full-time wolf didn't affect his ability to communicate with other wolves.

"I heard you the first time, Elliott. What are you doing here?" he asked, still staring into the distance, focusing on something.

"I was looking for you."

"Why?" he said harshly.

Elliott recoiled. Was he still angry about their fight at the funeral?

"I need your help with something," he said, walking closer to him.

He finally turned his head, staring at Elliott with his vibrant gold eyes. He sighed. "Brotherly advice, huh? Let me guess... it's about her?" He pointed his nose in the direction of the campus.

Elliott made his way around to sit at the edge of the hill with his brother. The woods stopped just past them, opening up to the college campus below.

"So, you know then," he said, lying down.

"Of course I know. I'm your brother."

"So Mom told you."

"Pretty much," Tristan said, turning to Elliott with a mischievous look in his eye.

"So then... what do you think I should do?"

"What do I think? Why would my opinion matter more than what everyone else is already telling you to do?"

"Because of..." He looked down, unsure whether mentioning Ava would upset him.

"Ava?"

"Yeah..."

"You're afraid that Dad will come after this girl like he did to Ava." He looked at Elliott sadly.

"Yes, I am."

Tristan sighed again. "Honestly, he probably already knows about her. Dad's just like that somehow, so there's no point in trying to hide anything from him. Besides, after the way things went with me after Ava died, I'd doubt he'd try the same thing with you. I'd say just go for it."

"Really?" he asked, surprised.

"Yeah. I mean, there's no use torturing yourself over not being with her. Dad's probably loving how much control he has over you, that bastard." He growled.

"Wow, so you're not worried about him at all, then?"

"Of course not! If anything, he should be worried that I'm going to come after him for what he's done." Tristan sank his claws into the ground and dragged them back in anger.

"So, you haven't seen him either since Ava died?"

"Only light traces of his scent here and there, never anything substantial. But hey, don't you worry about him. You should be worrying more about her saying no when you finally get the courage to ask her out."

"Ha ha. Very funny," Elliott said sarcastically.

"No, I'm serious. I had to ask Ava out like three different times before she finally took pity on me and said yes. Since humans don't have the same mating instinct we do, it's always possible it won't be reciprocated."

"Well, thanks for putting that new fear into my head." He whined, laying his head down on his paws.

"Oh, come on, you already knew this was a possibility!" Tristan said, pushing his muzzle up against Elliott's playfully.

"I know, but that was kind of the last thing on my mind before you brought it up!"

"Eh, I'm sure it'll be just fine. She seems like too nice of a girl to say no, anyway."

"So you basically brought that up to freak me out?"

"I wouldn't be your brother if I didn't get the chance to bother you every once in a while."

"Right," Elliott said, rolling his eyes.

"You know, Ava used to tell me that after she finally said yes and spent some time with me, she could tell something was different from her past boyfriends. So maybe humans do feel the same sort of bond we do, just to a lesser extent," he said sadly, looking up at the sky.

"That's probably just where they got the term 'soulmate' from,"

Elliott said.

Tristan simply nodded, and they sat there watching the students walk through the campus.

He caught sight of Mia walking back to her dorm with Thea, and his heart started pounding in his chest. He wanted to run to her immediately after talking to Tristan. He just wanted to be with her. No more trying to fool himself otherwise.

As his tail started smacking on the ground, Tristan's laugh echoed through his head.

"You're like a lovesick puppy!" he cried hysterically.

"Oh, shut it." Elliott pouted and looked away.

"I'm just so excited that my little bro is finally gonna be happy," he said, tackling him from the side.

They wrestled around through the trees before Elliott gave up, and they both walked back over to the clearing.

The two sat in silence for a while, just watching the students wander around campus. He missed spending time with his brother like he used to before he left for college.

"Hey, Tristan?"

"Yeah?"

"Why are you still running around out here? Why not just come back home?"

Tristan turned to look at him. "The human world has nothing for me now, and I refuse to give Dad the satisfaction of trying to get me to marry some pureblood girl of his choosing just to keep our family line pure."

"So then, why stick around town? Revenge?"

"No. To be honest, I was going to leave. But then I caught your scent as I was leaving. I couldn't figure out why you'd come back here, so I decided to stick around and see. Once Mom told me about your mate, I knew I had to stay."

"You stayed for me?"

"Yeah, I knew your dumb ass would need my help eventually."

Tristan nipped at his brother's ear, to which Elliott nipped him back. They both laughed at each other.

"Thanks, Tristan. I really needed this."

"Me too," he said, getting up. "I'd better get going, and you should, too."

"Yeah, you're probably right," he said, standing up.

"Hey, be careful out there. I've heard around that a bunch of members from packs around the East Coast have been disappearing recently, and I don't want to hear you've disappeared too."

"Thanks, I will."

Tristan started off back into the forest.

"Oh, hey, Tristan!" He turned back around to look at Elliott. "Don't be a stranger."

Tristan simply nodded before taking off into the woods.

Elliott ran back toward his car. The wind flowing through his fur felt like complete freedom. In some ways, he couldn't blame his brother for wanting to leave a world of responsibility behind just for this feeling.

As he ran, he felt a wave of clarity wash over him. Everything Tristan said was true. He shouldn't be afraid of his father because that was just playing into his hand. The next time he saw Mia, he was going to shoot his shot.

CHAPTER FIFTEEN

THE WEATHER WAS TURNING as fall finally arrived. The air felt crisp, and the leaves were fading into beautiful shades of red and orange. This was Mia's favorite time of year, and she often spent it outside in a cozy sweater, writing away in her journal with a cup of hot apple cider.

She now sat on a bench outside in the quad, scrawling away ideas in a notebook for future stories. So lost in her work, when her phone buzzed against the metal of the bench, she physically jumped.

She closed the notebook and put it next to her. Picking up her phone, she saw a text from Erika.

S.O.S.

Mia sighed and leaned her head back, lifting her glasses off and rubbing her eyes. An S.O.S. from Erika was never a good sign. When she opened her eyes again, Elliott was standing above her and she jumped again, her glasses falling out of her hand and behind the bench.

"Sorry, I didn't mean to startle you," he said sheepishly, picking them up.

"It's fine," she said as he came around the bench and took the spot next to her, handing her back her glasses.

"So, what's up? You looked like something was bothering you," he asked.

"It was just a text from Erika. It's an S.O.S, which could mean anything really, but definitely nothing good." She quickly sent a text back asking what was wrong.

"Well... hopefully it's not something too serious," he said nervously. He looked down and saw the notebook next to her. "Were you writing something?"

She picked the notebook up and quickly shoved it into her bag. "Yeah, but... it was nothing really... just some random ideas."

Elliott laughed at her reaction. "Think I'll ever get to read any of them?"

"Probably not. I don't even let Thea read my writing. Or Erika and Peter, whom I've known for years... or even my parents..." She trailed off.

"That's a pretty long list you've got there." He chuckled.

She just stared at him, trying to tell if he was joking or not. When he said nothing else, she decided that must have been all he had to say on the matter.

"So, was there a reason you came over here, or did you just want to say hi?" she asked.

"Oh, um... There was..." He seemed nervous, scratching the back of his head and looking around as if trying to find the courage to say something.

Mia raised her eyebrows at him. "Yes?"

"I, uh... wanted to ask you... if... if you'd like to go out with me sometime?" His face flushed a bright red.

Mia stared at him, dumbfounded, her heart racing faster than it ever had before. Was he being serious?

"I, um..." Her thoughts were running a mile a minute. She wanted this, right? The strange feeling in the pit of her stomach returned, a longing for him she just couldn't describe. But the logical part of her brain was screaming at her to say no.

"Mia?"

"Sorry, I just—this caught me off guard…" she stuttered as she played with her phone in her hands nervously. It buzzed with new messages from Erika.

"Hey, uh, if you're not sure, that's fine…" he said, disappointed. "I just thought—"

"N-no! Uh, I'm sorry," she cut him off hastily, waving her hands in the air. "I didn't mean to disappoint you. I'm just not very good with surprises and, uh—this was… this was definitely a surprise." She chuckled to herself and looked away, unable to meet his gaze without blushing.

"Oh," he said, shocked. "Really?"

"Yeah, I mean, to me at least." She looked at him sheepishly as her phone buzzed once more. "I'm sorry. I should really see what's got Erika all worked up."

She looked at her phone, furrowing her brow as she read Erika's texts.

"Oh yeah, of course, but um… Mia?"

"Yeah?" She looked back up at him. His eyes were wide and questioning.

"Your answer?"

That's right. What was her answer? Should she give in to that feeling and dive headfirst into a relationship that started out so strangely? Or should she be cautious like normal and give their friendship more time?

"I, uh…" She took a shaky breath, looking into his sparkling blue eyes. She knew her answer. "Sure." She nodded, letting a smile slide onto her face. "Yeah, I think I would like that."

Her heart was pounding so hard in her chest she felt it might just burst. She was really doing this!

"Awesome," he said, smiling back at her with even more enthusiasm. "Yeah, great! I'll, uh… I'll think of something and text you!" he said giddily before walking away.

He turned back and waved at her, almost running into another student in the process. She giggled at how silly he was acting. She'd never seen him like that before.

Though she was confused—most people planned a date before asking someone out, but he didn't. Was he that eager to ask her he hadn't given a thought to the date itself?

She wasn't sure why, but it brought a smile to her lips to know that he wanted to go out with her so badly he hadn't even made it to the planning portion of the date.

Her phone started ringing, interrupting her thoughts and reminding her she still hadn't responded to Erika.

She quickly picked up the phone.

"Hey, sorry I haven't responded. I was, uh… busy," she said, deciding it was best not to tell her about Elliott during whatever this crisis was.

"I sent an S.O.S! What do you mean you were too busy to answer it?" she demanded.

Same old Erika, always quick to get to the point.

"I was just about to respond to you. I saw Peter's name involved? What's going on?"

"Dani broke up with him!"

"Again? That's the big S.O.S?" She let out a deep breath. "They'll just be back together again in a few weeks."

"No, she was cheating on him, M. It's not good. He's crushed."

"Oh boy. That is a problem." She chewed on her nail nervously.

"Yeah, and I feel bad 'cause neither of us are there for him right now," Erika said. She could hear the remorse in her voice.

That's right; they were both away from home right now. She felt terrible that she couldn't be there for one of her dearest friends, and now her love life was just starting as his was ending.

"Well, we can do a video chat. Maybe do an online movie night thing where we all stream the same movie at the same time?" she offered.

"Yeah, maybe that could work," Erika said, not sounding too convinced.

"And we'll see him over Thanksgiving break, so we'll just have to comfort him then." It wasn't the greatest plan, but it was the best Mia could offer.

"Definitely. Oh, man, I've gotta get going. But make sure to text him or give him a call!"

"Will do!" she said as Erika hung up on her.

She leaned back on the bench and sighed. She felt bad about Peter. But the thought of her date with Elliott made her feel restless and giddy. With so many conflicting emotions, she needed to clear her head.

She got up and walked back to her dorm to talk to Thea.

He'd done it! He couldn't believe he'd done it! He asked her out, and she actually said yes! Elliott was positively ecstatic as he walked back to his car. He could hardly contain himself.

He immediately drove to the clearing where he normally entered the woods. Quickly stripping and placing his clothes into the tree stump he always used, he immediately shifted and took off in a sprint.

He howled in excitement and ran as fast as he could through the woods, just trying to get the excess energy out of his body.

Suddenly, he was tackled from the side by a smaller brown wolf, and the two of them went tumbling through the trees.

"Lucy!" Elliott shouted through their minds once they'd stopped tumbling.

She continued to wrestle him, which he gladly went along with, taking advantage of getting his pent-up energy out.

"Lucy, what are you doing here?" He laughed once it was clear he was the winner of their little wrestling match.

"Just needed to go for a little run." She snarled playfully.

"Does Mom know you're skipping classes?"

"It's just last period," she said, rolling over onto her back. "And what she doesn't know won't hurt her."

He scoffed at her. He would be lying if he said he never skipped classes to go for runs in high school. Being stuck in one spot all day long was aggravating.

"So, what are you doing out here? You're not one to go for day runs through the woods." She cocked her head to the side and looked at him disapprovingly. "And I heard you howling. You know better than to do that during the day, especially with those strange disappearances happening recently."

"Just had some pent-up energy I needed to get out," he said nonchalantly, looking away from her and out into the woods.

"Pent-up energy?" she questioned at her brother's odd tone.

"Yeah, I, uh… I did something a little crazy, and I felt like I needed a run."

"Sounded more like a celebration to me."

"Well..." he teased, standing up and stretching out his limbs.

"Oh, stop being so cryptic and just tell me already!" she demanded as she hopped up and circled him excitedly.

"I asked her out."

Lucy's eyes grew wide at the statement, and she started hopping up and down.

"You asked her out?" she said giddily, taking her turn to howl happily. "What did she say?"

"She said yes, obviously!" He dashed around the clearing, energy coursing through him all over again.

Lucy was squealing in his head and running in circles along with him.

"So, where are you taking her? The movies? A romantic dinner for two? I wanna know everything!"

Elliott stopped in his tracks. He hadn't even thought about what the actual date was going to be yet.

What was he going to do?

CHAPTER SIXTEEN

"THIS IS SO EXCITING! I can't believe my little Mia is going on a date!" Thea said excitedly, jumping with glee in front of her bed.

"Your 'little Mia'?" Mia questioned from across their dorm room, a sour look on her face at the nickname.

"Sorry, I'm just so excited for you!" she said as she hopped up onto her bed and grabbed a pillow to squeeze.

"Maybe more than me, even," Mia joked. She chuckled awkwardly, the excitement from before now becoming nothing but anxiety.

"Oh, come on, you have to be at least a little excited!"

"I mean, I'm still not sure what to think about all of this. He just asks me out of the blue to go out with him but never actually told me when and where it would be."

"Wait, he didn't tell you?"

Mia leaned up on her bed and looked at her hands in her lap.

"He said he'd think of something and text me. Which in itself seems a bit weird. Who asks someone out on a date but doesn't actually have a date in mind?"

"That is strange, but hey! Maybe that just means he was so excited to ask you out that he didn't even think that far ahead!"

"Hm, maybe," Mia said, leaning back on her bed again.

Her phone chimed, and she picked it up off her side table to see a text from Elliott.

"Is it him? It's totally him, isn't it?" Thea said, hopping off her bed and rushing over to Mia's side.

"Okay, you're way too giddy about all of this," she said.

"Sorry, I'll try to take it down a notch," Thea said, backing up towards her bed.

She waited in anticipation as Mia read the text message.

"So... what's it say?" Thea asked.

"He... wants me to meet him outside around four thirty and to, uh... dress warm?" She raised her eyebrow in confusion and reread the text again. There was no other information other than what to wear and where to meet.

"That's it?"

"That's all it says." She shrugged.

She stared at Thea as they both thought what it could be.

"Hm... maybe he's taking you on a picnic! Aw, that would be so cute!"

"That seems like the obvious choice to go with if he wants me to dress warm at the end of October."

"Well, let's not stand here guessing. We've gotta pick you out a cute fall outfit!"

"Oh, absolutely not. You are going nowhere near my wardrobe!"

Four thirty rolled around faster than Mia expected, and before she knew it, she was waiting in the lobby for Elliott to show up. Thea insisted on pulling Mia's hair back into a French braid as a compromise for letting Mia pick out her own outfit.

Her heart was racing, and she felt like her stomach was in knots as she waited for him to show up. She twisted the end of her hair nervously in her fingers, a habit she'd had since she was a little girl. Just sitting around like this always made her anxious, and she hadn't been on an actual date since her senior year of high school, which made the thought of going out now even worse.

She finally got up and walked outside to see if he was waiting there for her.

"Hey, Mia!" Elliott shouted.

She looked over to see him running towards her from the parking lot. She was glad to see she wasn't underdressed in her black cardigan over a purple long sleeve top, jeans, and combat boots. He was wearing a black sweatshirt and jeans as well.

"Hey!" she said, walking over to meet him halfway. "So, where are we headed?"

"Oh, it's a surprise!" he said, offering his elbow. She gladly wrapped her arm in his, and he led her to his car. "It's a good one, though, I promise."

He smiled at her like a child who had difficulty holding in a secret. She couldn't help but smile back at him.

"A surprise, huh? Sounds fun."

"It is a little hike to get there, though, so I hope you don't mind," he said sheepishly as he opened the car door for her before rounding the car and getting into the driver's seat.

"I'm down for anything." She shrugged.

"Excellent!" he said, turning on the car.

As he drove, she realized they were headed towards the hills on the outskirts of town. She'd never really explored this far out before since she wasn't really an outdoors person.

They drove for about ten minutes before coming to a stop at the edge of the woods. He really wasn't joking about having to hike to wherever he was taking her. The sun was going down, and she was nervous about walking through the woods in the dark.

"I promise it's worth it once you get to the top," he said once he saw her staring into the woods.

"Well… lead the way, then," she said, getting out of the car. "Is there a path or something we should take?"

"Only one that I've made myself." He chuckled. "But there's plenty of daylight left, and I'm here to show you the way, so don't be too worried about it."

He lifted his hand towards her to help guide her. She hesitantly took it, and when her hand touched his, she felt a tingle run up her fingers.

She stared down at her hand and then back up at him to find he was grinning at her. Did he feel that too?

She followed him through the woods hand-in-hand for almost ten minutes before the trees opened up into a big clearing.

Mia stopped walking and gasped as she took in the view. The hilltop looked out over the entire town, and the setting sun cast a warm glow over the buildings. There was a blanket set out near the edge of the clearing with a picnic basket sitting right next to it and a few unlit candles lying around. It was a perfect romantic setting.

Her heart started beating a million miles a minute at the thought of being alone with him up here.

"It's pretty, isn't it?" Elliott said as he walked over to the picnic basket.

"It's beautiful." Mia beamed. "I had no idea something like this was even up here."

"Not many people do." He pulled plates out from the picnic basket and set up some cheese and crackers. "This is kind of my own special spot. I used to come up here a lot during high school just to get away from my family."

"Well, I'm honored that you brought me here then," she joked, walking over to join him on the picnic blanket. "But what's so bad about your family that you'd need to sneak all the way out here?"

"My dad was just—well, is—a lot to deal with." He looked out over the horizon. "He's pretty much the whole reason I moved away from this place as soon as I graduated from high school."

"That explains why we've never met before this year."

"Did I... never mention that to you before?" he asked, cocking his head to the side.

"Not that I can recall. We usually only talk about Duel of Ages, or whatever new comic is out. I don't think we've ever really talked about ourselves."

Mia was actually grateful for that fact. She never knew what to say when it came to her own personal life.

He thought about it for a moment. "Is that why you were so surprised when I asked you out?"

"Yeah... I guess so." She paused for a moment, thinking. "I just have a thing about getting to know someone before I really like them. I kind of forget it's not the same for everyone. I didn't even realize you liked me like that..." She wasn't sure why she was telling him so much. She just couldn't help but blurt out whatever came to her mind now that she was around him. "I mean, the only thing I had to go on was that stupid bet Mia, Zeke, and your sister had going. But that wasn't a total way of knowing how you actually felt."

He looked startled at her mention of the bet.

"Wait, you knew about the bet?" he asked, surprised.

"Yeah. Thea keeps nothing from me, unfortunately. I wasn't real happy to hear about it. I'm guessing you knew about it too, then?"

"Yup, Zeke told me." He chuckled. "Not a clue why, though. He probably had some ulterior motive, knowing him."

"Ulterior motive for starting the bet, or for telling you about it?"

"Telling me. He probably thought he could convince me to ask you out sooner or something." He scratched his head and looked away sheepishly.

Just how long had he wanted to ask her out? He talked like it had been for a long time, and yet he waited until now. Once again, his actions confused her, but at the same time she was intrigued.

"Why—why would you need convincing?" she asked hesitantly.

"Oh, uh… Well, after everything that happened after we first met, I wasn't really sure…" He trailed off, unsure of what to say.

"You weren't sure what I thought of you?"

"Yes," he whispered, pulling his legs up to his chest and placing his chin on top of them.

She stared at him for a moment.

"So then… What made you decide now was the time?"

He looked back up at her and let a small smile come to his face.

"I decided waiting to figure you out was taking too long."

She laughed and smacked him playfully on the arm.

"I'm not that complicated! And it's not like you're an open book either. Besides talking about our game nights and comic books, I don't know a lot about you as a person."

"Well, dating is all about getting to know each other. So, what is it you want to know about me?"

He pulled out a plate of finger sandwiches from the picnic basket and placed them on the blanket.

His question caught her off guard. What did she want to know about him? So many questions crossed her mind, but what was it she wished to know most?

"I can go first if you can't think of anything right away," he said when she didn't immediately ask him something.

He grabbed a sandwich off the plate and took a bite, waiting for her to answer.

"Hm..." Suddenly it struck her. "Why did you come back to town if you hate it here so much?"

Elliott choked on his sandwich and turned ghostly pale. That made Mia even more curious to hear what his answer was, but he was clearly distraught about the question.

"You don't have to answer that if it's too personal. I can always ask something else," she said, concerned.

"N-no, you don't have to do that. It's just… the reason isn't really, uh… a happy one."

"Oh?" She turned towards him.

"Yeah. Uh, my sister-in-law was in a car crash over the summer and she… she didn't make it."

"Oh my gosh, I'm so sorry, Elliott." She breathed out.

Now she thoroughly regretted asking him that question.

"Oh, thank you for your concern, but you don't have to feel bad for asking about it," he said, giving her a sad smile. "I wasn't entirely close with her. Sure, it was upsetting, but it's been a few months, so I'm over the grieving stage. I mainly came back because my mom asked me to."

"Well… it's still sad to hear about." She turned her head to look at the sunset.

It was beginning to get dark, and Elliott pulled out a lighter from the picnic basket.

"So, anyway, my turn for a question," he said as he started lighting the candles. "Do you have any siblings?"

"Nope, just me. Guess my parents thought just one of me was enough." She laughed, taking a cracker and a slice of cheese.

"Having siblings isn't all it's cracked up to be, believe me." He joked.

"Oh, I know. Erika has, like, three other sisters, and growing up around them made me appreciate being an only child." She chuckled, and he laughed with her.

She grabbed a sandwich and took a bite.

"It's your turn to ask a question," he said, smiling at her.

"Oh, right." She finished chewing. "Hm… let's see… oh! What do you wanna be when you grow up?"

"When I grow up?" He let out a small laugh. "I'm already twenty. Does that not count as grown up?"

"Technically, you're still growing until you're twenty-five, so…"

"Then, I guess… Hmm, I guess I'd like to own a restaurant. Maybe be a chef there."

"A chef?"

"Yeah, can't you tell by this wonderful spread I put together?" he said sarcastically, gesturing to the picnic.

She giggled. "Oh, definitely."

"Seriously, though, you should let me make something for real sometime. Y'know, when I actually have time to prepare something properly."

"Are you asking me out on a second date before we're even done with the first one?" she teased.

"That depends… Would you say yes if I was?"

"Hm." She dramatically placed a finger on her chin as she thought about it.

Despite her anxiety before he arrived, she now felt completely comfortable around him. Almost like a switch had flipped inside her and she couldn't think of not being with him.

"I think I just might," she said with a grin.

A smile spread across his face, and he turned away from her out of embarrassment.

Her heart skipped a beat when she saw it, and the butterflies immediately returned to her stomach, only this time she didn't think to shove them away.

"So, anyway…" Mia started. "I believe it's your turn to ask a question."

CHAPTER SEVENTEEN

IT WAS THE FIRST full moon since Elliott had his date with Mia, and he felt awful about canceling on her for it. He knew this would be a secret he would have to keep for a while, until she was ready to hear it, but it still felt like a complete betrayal to not tell her the real reason they couldn't hang out tonight.

He walked into the woods, hiding his clothes in his usual tree trunk, and waited for the moon to rise. He hated full moons—not having the control to shift when he wanted to felt like he was a prisoner in his own body.

And then it happened. He yelped out in pain as the moon forced him to change into a wolf for the rest of the night. His bones snapped and reformed against his will, his body fighting him as his limbs elongated, and fur sprouted all over his body. Once he had shifted and his senses were heightened, he immediately knew something was wrong. Something smelled rotten...

"Hello, Elliott," his father said, stalking out through the trees. His blue eyes almost glowed in the dark against his hulking figure of black fur. Those blue eyes he loathed to have inherited.

"What do you want?" He growled.

"What, no hello for your dear old dad?" he asked sarcastically as he slowly circled him.

"You don't deserve a hello after what you've done."

"Oh, Elliott, when did you come to be so spiteful towards me?" he asked, feigning offense.

Elliott neglected to answer. He crouched low and continued to growl.

"Well then, I suppose any formalities we could've had are gone." He pounced towards Elliott, narrowly missing him as Elliott jumped away. "Why have you come back, after all this time?"

"For Mom, for Tristan, because you ripped his life apart."

"Ah yes, your brother. How disgraceful that'd he'd rather stay in this form than continue on our family line," he said, not denying his involvement in Ava's death.

"He's only doing that because of you!" Elliott jumped at his father, missing by a few feet.

"You've become rather judgmental, blaming me for things without getting my side of the story."

"Enlighten me then. What did happen?"

"I was simply passing through. It's not my fault that little human didn't know how to swerve around something without crashing," he said coldly.

A blur came through the trees and the next thing Elliott knew, his dad was rolling, and in a fit of snarls and growls, he saw Tristan.

"Poor little Tristan," his father taunted, dodging Tristan's bite's. "All heartbroken and alone."

"Leave him alone!" Elliott leapt at his father, managing to separate the two of them. He stood in between them, so neither side could make a move against the other without hurting him.

"Move, Elliott. He deserves to die for what he's done!" Tristan spat.

"Oh, always with the dramatics, Tristan," his father said.

"Remember what I told you boys when you were younger about the bond? It only leads to heartbreak." He looked directly at Elliott.

Elliott growled low at his father's warning.

"You're wrong!" Tristan spat. "I was happy, and you're the only reason that happiness is gone!"

"If that's what you'd like to think, then fine," his father said, walking closer to Elliott and looking him straight in the eye. "I just hope you've learned from your brother's mistake."

Elliott let out another growl, and his father laughed. It was a cold and unfeeling laugh that made Elliott's fur stand on end.

"Don't you worry about your little pet, Elliott. You can have your fun with her for now, but after the winter, it'll be time to get serious about your future, and she won't be in it," his father said before running off into the woods.

"Don't worry, Elliott, I'll make sure nothing happens to her," Tristan said, chasing after their father.

Elliott always knew his father had a way of finding things out. Tristan even told him so. But it wasn't until now, until this confirmation, that he was truly fearing for Mia's life.

It had been a few days since Elliott canceled their date, and he still hadn't responded to any of her texts. He was only supposed to be spending some time with his family, so did something happen, or was it her? She couldn't help but feel extremely self-conscious.

She was waiting outside the building of his class to confront him about it, her mind racing with the possibilities of what could be wrong. He knew better than to ignore her, especially given how they met, so something had to have caused him to act like this.

Finally, he made his way outside, looking lost in his own thoughts.

"Hey, Elliott!" Mia shouted, running up to him as he was

leaving the history building.

He jumped, startled by her sudden appearance. Mia didn't think she'd ever seen him jump like that. Somehow, he'd always heard her coming.

"Oh, hey, Mia, what's up?" he asked almost solemnly.

They walked out into the quad, and Mia could tell something was definitely wrong. She figured it was better she ease her way into asking him about it.

"So… how was your family night this weekend?"

"Oh, it was… it was okay… I guess," he stuttered, keeping his eyes forward and not looking at her.

"Okay…" Mia said. "Well, are we still on for a movie night tonight? Thea's got her club meeting, and then they usually all go out for food afterwards, so she won't be back until late."

"I, uh… I don't know. I've got quite a bit of homework and studying to do…"

"On a Monday?"

"Yeah, I'm not really good at keeping up with my work like you are." He forced out a small chuckle, and it pained Mia to hear it.

She could tell he was making excuses not to hang out with her, but why? Had she done something wrong? Did he not like her anymore? That would be her luck, of course. She had finally felt a greater connection with him, and now he was pulling away from her.

"Elliott…" She stopped walking. "Are you all right?"

He turned around to face her, smiling awkwardly. "Yeah, I'm totally fine."

He still wasn't making eye contact with her.

"Then… why are you canceling on me again? It kind of seems like you don't really want to be around me right now…"

He looked at her, hurt that she had accused him of such a thing. From the month she'd been with him, she'd learned he was definitely not good at hiding his emotions.

"It's not that, I promise!" He grabbed her hands and looked

into her eyes.

"Then what is it?" She pulled her hands out of his and wrapped her arms nervously around herself. "Did something happen Saturday night? Because that's the last time you even texted me, and normally we talk everyday, so—"

"I'm sorry, Mia. I know I've been acting weird. It's just..." He paused, and it looked like he was searching for the right thing to say. He sighed before continuing. "My dad showed up Saturday night, and it's the first time I've seen him in, like, two and a half years."

"Oh," she said, understanding. He'd told her all about his father, how controlling he was over every decision Elliott made. Especially when it came to his relationships. It was no surprise that he'd keep to himself after seeing him again.

"It was just... not a great talk I had with him, and he and Tristan got into a big fight—"

"Wait, Tristan, as in your older brother? I thought you'd said he left town," she interrupted.

He winced, almost as if he wasn't supposed to mention that.

"O-Oh... yeah, he did," he said nervously. "He was only back in town this weekend to see my mom. That's why it was so important for me to go over there," he practically sputtered out.

Mia squinted her eyes at him, unsure if she wanted to believe such an obviously fabricated response, but what reason would he have for lying to her about something like that?

"Anyway, I haven't really been in the best mindset since I saw him. I'm sorry, I really haven't been meaning to be so distant." He looked at her sadly.

She let out a breath she didn't know she was holding. "I understand. Thank you for being so honest with me. I'm sorry for prying so much. I just get worried sometimes..." She trailed off, not wanting to admit how self-conscious she actually was.

"Well, how about this then..." he said, thinking. "Why don't you come over for dinner next weekend? You could finally meet my mom and stepdad."

"Next weekend? As in over Thanksgiving break?"

"Is that really next weekend?" he asked, astonished.

"Uh… yeah!" She chuckled.

"Wow, time really flies. My offer still stands, though."

She thought about it for a minute. She was supposed to see Erika and Peter, but maybe they'd be okay just seeing each other on Friday. And she doubted her parents would oppose her going out on a date. They were as excited as Thea was to hear there was a boy in her life now.

"I suppose I could come back early," she said.

"Then it's a date!" He smiled at her for real this time, his warm demeanor immediately coming back. She swore every time she saw that smile, it made her fall harder for him.

"It's a date." She smiled back.

He draped his arm around her shoulder and walked her back to her dorm.

CHAPTER EIGHTEEN

MIA PULLED INTO THE driveway at Elliott's mother's house, incredibly nervous to be meeting her for the first time. Usually, meeting someone's parents meant they were getting serious. Did Elliott really think of her that way so soon?

Elliott stepped out onto the wrap-around porch before she even turned off her car. Seeing him made her immediately smile, and her nervousness dissipated.

"Hey, Mia!" he yelled, waving enthusiastically as she got out of her car.

She waved back at him and started walking towards the house. As she got near the steps, she slipped on ice, and he was down the stairs to catch her before she even knew what was happening.

"I'm sorry, I should have warned you about the black ice!" he said frantically.

"Oh, it's fine. I hadn't even realized it was cold enough for ice yet." She laughed as he helped her back to her feet. "Though this catching me thing is becoming quite a theme with us, and I'm not even usually that clumsy."

He thought about that for a moment. "You know, now that I think about it, this is the third time I've had to catch you like this since we've met."

The two of them laughed, forgetting that they were standing out in the chilly November weather.

"Okay, you lovebirds, are you coming in to eat or not?" Lucy said sarcastically. She was leaning on the doorframe of the house with her arms crossed.

"Oh, hey, Lucy, how are you?" Mia asked, blushing at the mention of her and Elliott being "lovebirds."

"I'm doing just fine! Good to finally see you again!" She looked over at Elliott. "Maybe you should bring her inside before she freezes to death," she joked before turning around and walking back into the house.

Mia moved to follow Lucy inside, but Elliott grabbed her arm.

"Before we go inside, I wanted to give you something," he said sheepishly as she turned back towards him. He pulled a long box out of the pocket of his hoodie.

"Oh?" she asked, looking down at the box in his hand. It was dark blue and wrapped in bright white ribbon, tied together at the top with a beautiful crescent moon charm hanging off of it.

"It's not much, but… I wanted to apologize for the way I was acting last weekend," he said as he handed over the box.

Mia smiled as she slowly unwrapped the ribbon, careful not to lose the moon charm. As she lifted the cover off of the box, she let out a small gasp.

Inside lay a beautiful necklace. A silver cage in the shape of a heart was attached to a long chain. She pulled the necklace out to inspect the charm closer to see that there was a pink stone inside.

"It's, um… rose quartz inside. I was told it was a good stone to give you…" he said nervously.

"Oh, Elliott, it's beautiful!" Mia said as she slipped the chain over her head. The charm landed midway down her chest. "Thank you so much," she said with a warm smile, grabbing his hand and squeezing it.

"I'm glad you like it." He smiled back at her, leaving butterflies fluttering in her stomach. They stood there staring into each other's eyes, a contemplating look painted on Elliott's face.

He slowly closed the space between them, brushing a stray strand of hair off Mia's face. Her cheek tingled at his touch, and she could feel her face flush. He leaned his head down towards hers.

"Can you two hurry it up? You're letting the cold in!" Lucy shouted from in the house.

They both let out a nervous laugh.

"I guess we should head in, then," Mia said breathlessly.

"Yeah..." Elliott said sadly at their ruined moment. He took her hand and led her inside.

The front door opened up into a beautiful living room. There was a large fireplace, which had a flat screen TV mounted to the wall above it, and a Christmas tree had already been put up in the corner of the room, despite it only being two days after Thanksgiving.

Lucy was sitting on the couch watching a reality show when they walked in.

"'Bout time you two came inside. Now close the door, Elliott; it's freezing out there!" she said.

"You could've done that yourself instead of waiting for us," he mumbled as he closed the door behind Mia. She couldn't help but let out a small chuckle at their banter.

"Dinner's almost ready. Why don't you help set the table, Lucy," Elliott's mother called, walking into the living room.

"Will do, Mom!" Lucy said, hopping off the couch and shutting off the TV before running down the hallway towards the kitchen.

Elliott's mother locked eyes with Mia. "Oh! You must be Mia!"

She walked over, and Mia reached her hand out to shake his mother's, but she went for a hug instead.

"It is so lovely to finally meet you, dear!" she said, squeezing the breath out of Mia.

"It's nice to meet you too!" Mia managed to choke out.

Mia locked eyes with Elliott, who was grinning like a fool. He mouthed "I'm sorry" to her right before his mother released her from the hug.

She smiled warmly at Mia, and her brown eyes sparkled with love.

"Why don't you two wait in the dining room?" She gestured to the door on her left. "We're almost done with everything, so it shouldn't be too long now."

"Thanks, Mom, I'll show her the way," Elliott said.

He brought her into the dining room where a long table sat. A gorgeous orange and red centerpiece had been placed in the middle, left over from their Thanksgiving festivities. Cabinets full of fine china filled the sides of the room, with family photos set up on top of them.

"Sorry, I should have warned you that my mom was a hugger," Elliott said as she took in the room.

"Oh, it's fine. She just caught me off guard." Mia laughed.

She walked farther into the room, staring at the three senior portraits that hung on the wall. Lucy was in the middle, all smiley and bubbly, with her hair done up in beautiful waves that framed her lightly freckled face perfectly. Elliott was on the left, smiling with his mouth closed and his eyes looking unhappy, and on the right...

"Is this Tristan?" Mia asked, pointing to the photo. He looked a lot like Elliott, his hair dark and bushy, but his eyes were a warm caramel color and not the striking blue his brother had. His face was also more angular compared to Elliott's rounder cheeks.

"Yup, that's him," he said, walking over and standing next to her, staring up at the photo.

"He looks a lot like you, except for the eyes... and his smile is different, too."

"He was lucky enough to get my mom's eyes, unlike me."

"Oh, don't say that. I like your blue eyes!" she said, meandering her way over to the baby photos placed on top of a cabinet nearby. "Awww, look at this one!"

She picked up a photo of Elliott's mother in front of a carousel. A little boy on her right clung to her leg while a girl with dark, wild hair stood triumphantly on her left. In her arms, she held a tiny baby.

"So, this is Tristan, right?" she said, pointing to the little boy. "Is that you as a baby?"

He took the photo from her and stared at it. "Yeah, it is."

"Aw, you were so cute!" she teased. "So, who's this girl, your cousin?"

"No, she's um..." He put the photo down. "She's my older sister," he said sadly, looking away from her.

"You have an older sister?" she said, surprised. Why had he never mentioned her before?

"Had. I had an older sister. She ran away when I was younger..." He ruffled his hair and looked away from her. "We never found her..."

"Oh, Elliott..." she said sadly.

"Just don't mention it around my mom, okay?" He looked back at her with sad eyes. "She never quite healed from that."

"Of course. I completely understand," she said, grabbing his hand for support.

She felt so bad for his family. First, he lost his sister, then his sister-in-law all these years later, mixed with his overbearing father... it was a wonder he could still smile at her the way he did.

"Hey, I'm sorry for prying. I shouldn't have—" she started.

"No, it's fine. How could you have known?" he reassured her. "Besides, someday I'll get to meet your parents and it'll be my turn to pry," he said, smiling mischievously.

She elbowed him in the arm, and they both laughed.

"Hope you're starving, because we've got way too much food for just the five of us!" Lucy said as she walked in the room carrying a basket of crescent rolls with butter balanced on top in one hand

and a bowl of cooked vegetables in the other.

Lucy was not exaggerating. Every time Mia thought they were done bringing things to the table, another dish came out of the kitchen.

"I wasn't sure what you liked, so I just made a bunch," his mother said.

"And she wouldn't even let me help." Elliott pouted.

Mia laughed. "Well, at least that means there will be plenty of leftovers later."

"That's true! And take as much as you want. This dinner is for you, after all," his mother said.

"Oh, you're too kind!" Mia said.

They chatted the evening away, Mia feeling like she was part of the family. Elliott's mother was kind, and Mia wondered if she treated every person who came into her home like they were her own child. His stepfather was quiet and reserved, but she could tell he was happy as long as Elliott was. And Lucy was as energetic as always. She spent the entire night egging on her brother and trying to make Mia laugh. It was truly wonderful. She couldn't think of a time in her life when she was happier.

It almost made Mia sad when it came time for her to leave. Elliott's mother was sending her off with three containers full of leftovers, which she couldn't complain about. Though Thea would probably end up eating most of it.

"Thank you so much for having me tonight! The food was delicious. I'm sorry I didn't eat more!" Mia said.

"Oh, don't you even worry about that! I'm just happy we finally got to meet you!" his mother said, pulling her in for another hug.

Mia almost lost a hold on her leftovers but caught them as soon as she pulled away from the hug.

His mom put her hands on Mia's shoulders. "Don't be a stranger," she said before walking back into the kitchen to clean up.

"Well, I guess that means it's time for me to walk you to your car," Elliott said, opening the front door while balancing the other two boxes of food in his other hand. "After you."

As she walked outside, the sudden cold nipped at Mia's face, sending a chill down her spine. Elliott placed his free arm around her as they walked. He looked out into the dark woods across the street with a worried look on his face, as if he was searching for something.

"You all right?" she asked.

He shook his head lightly before looking back at her and smiling.

"Yeah... I'm fine," he said. "So, did you have a good time tonight?" he asked once they reached her car.

"I did! Your family is very welcoming. I think I enjoyed them more than my own family gatherings." Mia laughed.

He chuckled. "That's good to hear, because I just thought they were embarrassing."

"I think everyone thinks of their family like that."

"Probably..." He looked around awkwardly. "So, are you headed back to campus?"

"Yeah, no point in going all the way back home just to drive back tomorrow night," she said, unlocking the car and walking to the passenger's side to put her leftovers on the seat. "You wanna come keep me company tomorrow until Thea gets back?"

"I'd love to," he said as she rounded back to the driver's side of the car.

"Great! I'll see you tomorrow then!" She opened the door to get in her car.

"Uh... Mia?" Elliott said nervously.

"Hm?"

She turned around, and his face was bright red. She wasn't sure if it was the cold or if he was just blushing.

"Are you okay?" she asked him.

"I... um..." He looked away from her. When he turned back again, he had a serious look on his face.

He cupped her cheeks in his hands, heat rising to her face as he leaned down and kissed her.

It was electrifying; she had never felt a kiss like this before. It was like everything she had ever wanted was right there with him. She belonged there; she was safe there.

She leaned in towards him, deepening the kiss when he suddenly pulled away. As soon as she did, she felt the need to kiss him again, to never let him go.

"I've been wanting to do that for a while now," he confessed.

"I'm glad you didn't wait any longer," she said, pulling him down into another kiss.

When they finally parted again, it made her sad. Leaving him always made her feel empty, something she learned to just deal with, even if it wasn't normal.

"You should get going," he said, eyes never leaving hers.

"Probably…" she said, not wanting to go.

"Until tomorrow," he said, stepping away so she could finally leave and get some rest.

"Until tomorrow." She smiled, getting into her car.

As she drove, she clutched the heart charm of the necklace he gave her. It gave her a sense of comfort, almost like he was there with her, making their parting easier than before. She smiled again at the thought of their kiss.

That wonderful, beautiful kiss.

CHAPTER NINETEEN

WINTER BREAK HAD FINALLY come, and the weather was beyond cold. There was a fresh dusting of snow on the ground, which really made it feel like the start of the holiday season.

Mia usually loved coming home for the winter break, but this time was different. Now, she had Elliott. She felt safer when he was around, and for some reason now that he wasn't with her for this month-long break, she couldn't help but feel uneasy. She was happy to be seeing her friends from home and her family again, but she felt like there was something missing without Elliott here.

Lost in thought once again, Mia grabbed a heavy unmarked box from Peter's moving truck. She was beginning to regret agreeing to help him move into his new place, but that's what she got for skipping out on seeing him during the Thanksgiving break. Erika made her feel so guilty about it that she couldn't possibly say no when he asked for her help.

"Are we almost done yet?" Erika groaned, turning the corner onto the truck. She had her short, fluffy brown hair pushed back out of her face with a red fleece headband. Her tan skin was flecked with pink around her nose and ears. She had to have been just as cold as Mia was, despite the two of them doing all the heavy lifting.

"Not even close," Mia said, struggling to keep hold of the box she was carrying. Erika walked over and grabbed the other end, hoisting it up and helping Mia to carry it off the truck.

"Ugh, how does he even own so much? I don't even have this much to my name!" Erika complained as they headed towards the house.

"To be fair, you share a lot with your sisters."

"I know, but still. And where is he, anyway? I haven't seen him in, like, three trips to this truck."

They walked inside and dropped the box on the couch in front of the window.

It was small, but nice and cozy inside his new home. It was only one floor, but the living room was large, with the kitchen separated only by a countertop. Down a long hallway on the left was the bathroom and two bedrooms.

"Peter!" Erika shouted as she walked farther into the house. "Where the hell are you, and why are Mia and I doing all the work here?"

"Hang on a second, I'll be right out!" he yelled from one of the bedrooms.

"Y'know, he's probably just setting up his room," Mia said. "That's what I'd be excited to do if I was moving into a new place all by myself."

"You're too nice, Mia. New room or not, the least he could do is help us empty this truck of all his shit before he starts playing interior designer." She crossed her arms, annoyed.

"Making fun of me when I'm not around again, Erika?" Peter said, walking out of the hallway while adjusting his glasses.

"Only because you deserve it," Erika joked back at him.

"Where did you want this box?" Mia asked, pointing to the one they just brought in. "It's not labeled or anything."

"Eh, just leave it there. I'll see what's in it later," he said.

"So, you gonna put your coat back on and help us get the rest of these boxes out or what? It's already almost three, and I'd kind of like to be done sometime in the next year," Erika said.

"All right, all right, message received," he said, grabbing his coat from the kitchen counter and placing a hat over his curly blonde hair.

It had taken them a while, but they were finally close to emptying the moving truck. Mia felt uneasy standing in the near empty truck by herself, and an icy chill ran down her spine. She grabbed the charm of the necklace Elliott gave her for comfort before hastily grabbing a box and practically running with it towards the house.

Suddenly, she felt eyes on the back of her head. She spun around to see a man standing there. His hair was dark and slicked back. He wore a large jacket and a blood-red scarf that covered most of his face. She couldn't tell if he was actually built like a bear, or if that was just his coat, but she didn't think it was a good idea to find out.

His bright blue eyes bore into her, and she couldn't help but want to be anywhere but there at that moment.

She was afraid to look away from him. She couldn't figure out why, but she had the strangest feeling he would come after her if she dared look away. Instead, she quickly backed towards the house, keeping her eyes on him the whole time.

"Hey, Mia, watch where you're goin'!" Peter said on his way out of the house when she almost ran into him.

"Get back inside!" she hastily whispered.

"What? Why?" he questioned, following her.

Erika was lounging on the couch, already done with helping Peter out.

"What's going on?" she asked, sitting up.

Peter shut the front door, and Mia placed the box she was holding on the ground.

"There's a man out there watching us!" Mia whispered, distressed.

"What?" Erika said, turning towards the window as Peter went over to look.

"Don't make it obvious!" Mia pulled Peter away from the window.

"He does look pretty sketchy…" Erika said.

"Oh, he's probably just some nosey neighbor looking to see who's moving in," Peter said, never quick to judge someone.

"No, he's giving me some bad vibes, Peter. It's like I could feel his eyes boring into me!" Mia shuddered.

"Well, he's gone now," Erika said. Mia and Peter both turned to look out the window.

She was right. He had disappeared without a trace.

"Well, Peter, I really hope he's not a neighbor of yours; otherwise, you're not gonna see me around here a lot," Mia said, walking over and sitting on the couch next to Erika.

"Oh, come on, Mia," Peter said, rolling his eyes.

"No, I'm serious. He freaked me out!" She hugged herself, and Erika rubbed her on the back comfortingly.

"She's right, Pete, something was definitely off with that one," Erika said.

"Well, great, now you've both got me all paranoid!" he said. "Would you guys mind staying the night just so I know nothing weird's gonna go down?"

Erika sighed. "You could've just said you'd be lonely in this big place all by yourself."

"That's not what I said!" he shouted.

"It's what you meant to say," she egged him on.

"Come on, Erika, stop teasing him." Mia laughed. "We were planning on staying over, anyway."

"Aw, I knew I could count on you two!" he said, plopping himself in between them on the couch and pulling them in for a hug.

They finished getting the last of the boxes out of the truck, and after returning it, settled in for a night of pizza and board games.

It was a nice distraction, but deep down, Mia still felt uneasy. Like that man was still out there, watching her and waiting for something to happen.

CHAPTER TWENTY

MIA AND ELLIOTT SAT in her parents' living room. It was much smaller than his mother's place, but he felt that just made it even more cozy to live in.

There was a bookcase built into the wall, filled to the brim with novels of all kinds. He supposed that's where Mia got her love of writing from. Photos of her all throughout her life littered the room. Of course, being an only child, her parents wanted to put up memories of her everywhere they could. He could tell they loved her very much, even without getting the chance to meet them just yet.

He shifted in his spot on the couch, pulling her closer so she was on top of him.

"Are you even comfortable?" She laughed.

"More than you'd think," he said, resting his head on top of hers to watch the end of her favorite superhero movie.

They had the house completely to themselves while her parents were out at work, and he was more than grateful for that.

He was on edge because of the full moon tomorrow night, and

on top of that, Tristan had informed him that he spotted his dad nearby a few weeks ago. He definitely didn't want to make a bad impression on her parents because he was being "moody," as Lucy liked to put it.

"Elliott?" Mia asked, looking up at him.

"Hm?" he hummed, looking down at her. He barely heard her say his name. He was so focused on his own thoughts.

"I asked if you were good? The movie ended like two minutes ago and you're staring at the credits like they're the best part." She giggled.

"Sorry, I didn't realize."

"So, what's on your mind, then?"

"Oh, nothing important," he said sarcastically. "Just thinking about how unfair it is that you didn't let me snoop through all of your childhood photos," he joked.

"You were not thinking that!" she said, sitting up and slapping his arm playfully.

"How would you know? Are you psychic?"

She laughed at him. "No, but it sure would help if I was! Now tell me the truth!"

"Okay, okay," he said, catching his breath from laughing. "I was just thinking about how much I don't want to leave you again. I've missed you too much this past month."

He pulled her close, and she laughed as he buried his face in her neck, inhaling her sweet scent of cinnamon cookies.

It wasn't a complete lie; he missed her incredibly. He worried about her every single day she wasn't near him. Without her there, he just felt empty.

He never knew how much he was missing before she came into his life, and with his father's threat to take her away before winter's end, he couldn't help but want to keep her close.

"I've missed you too," she said, pulling him into a kiss.

She had become a lot more comfortable with him after their kiss over Thanksgiving break. Almost like she realized this was real, that she didn't have to be afraid of getting close to him.

And he enjoyed it. He enjoyed getting to know her more and getting to kiss her more. He loved kissing her. The sweet taste of her lips and her scent wrapping around him. He pulled her in closer, feeling her warm body there against his. He felt whole. He felt complete.

She pulled away from him, making him feel cold again.

"But you know, the break ends in two weeks, so we'll be back together again before you even know it," she said, attempting to cheer him up.

"I know. Still doesn't stop me from missing you," he said, kissing her forehead.

"Well, there's no use missing me while I'm right here. So, what do you say? Got time for another movie before you head home?"

He gave her a smile. "I've got all the time in the world if it's with you."

CHAPTER TWENTY-ONE

THE TWO WEEKS PASSED quickly, and before she knew it, Mia was on the road back to campus. She decided to drive back the night before Thea did so she could spend some time alone with Elliott.

"I'm almost to campus now, maybe like five or ten minutes," Mia said.

She had spent the entire ride back talking with Elliott on the phone. Even though he had just seen her two weeks ago, it seemed like he was eager to see her again.

"Sounds good. I'll head over now, and I'll help you carry your stuff inside," he said, and she heard rustling around in the background.

Mia laughed. "You say that like I have a lot of stuff to bring in."

"Well, how would I know? It's not like I'm psychic!" he joked.

"Ha ha, hilarious," she said, hearing Elliott's car start up in the background. "I'm going to beat you there if you're just leaving your place now."

"Only if you're speeding."

"I think you misjudge how far away I am."

"Or you did." He chuckled. "Did you forget I've lived in this town my whole life?"

"Doesn't mean you know everything about it!" She turned onto the road for the campus. "Anyway, I'm almost there, pulling into the campus now."

"I'd probably be a lot closer if I didn't hit every red light on the way there."

She could hear him tapping his steering wheel impatiently as he waited for the light to change.

Mia laughed at him. "Maybe you wouldn't have hit them if you left before I told you I was five minutes away."

She pulled into the parking lot of her dorm building and picked a spot close to the entrance.

"Huh, no one's around. Guess I'm the only one who wanted to come back early from break," she said, turning off the car and grabbing her phone off the stand of the dashboard.

She got out of the car and went to open the back door.

"Mia, I'm almost there. Just wait for me before getting your stuff," he said with an anxious tone in his voice.

"Too late, I'm already grabbing my duffle bag," she said, leaning into the car.

"Please, Mia, I'd just feel safer if you were in the car," he begged.

"Elliott, there's no one even around. Nothing's gonna happen to me."

She shut the car door and turned around, coming face-to-face with a beautiful blonde girl. Her hair was long, falling in waves, and she wore a stylish red coat with a fur trim. She looked almost like she could be a supermodel, but what was most striking about her was her blood-red eyes.

She was mere inches from Mia's face.

Mia opened her mouth to scream, but before she got the chance, the girl put a finger over Mia's mouth and whispered, "Sleep."

Suddenly, Mia felt exhausted.

"Mia?" Elliott said frantically over the phone.

She felt the world slipping away as her eyes struggled to stay open.

"Elliott?" she mumbled as her hand dropped to her side.

She heard her phone hit the pavement, Elliott's screaming mere noise in her ears before she fell to the ground, and everything went black.

"Mia?" Elliott yelled frantically.

He could tell something was wrong. He heard her gasp, and then nothing.

"Mia!" he shouted again, pressing on the gas. He didn't care how fast he was going. He needed to get to her.

"Elliott?" he heard her mumble before the phone sounded like it fell on the ground.

"Mia, please! Stay with me! Mia!" No matter how much he shouted, she never responded.

Something was terribly, terribly wrong.

He should have left sooner. Should have been there for her.

He knew his father was around, knew he was waiting for her.

Tristan even said he saw his father in the area, but he promised he was on it. Promised he would help keep her safe.

His car whipped into the parking lot, pulling up right next to hers.

He ripped his car door open and ran around to her driver's side where he found her phone and duffle bag lying on the ground, but no Mia.

He sniffed the air for her scent, but it was mixed with something strange that he couldn't place. Along with that unusual mask of smell, there was a hint of death mixed with rose perfume. It was a vampire that had taken her.

He ran to the woods as fast as possible and stripped off his clothes, immediately shifting into his wolf form to see if he could catch her scent better.

It was faint in the air. He followed it as far as he could, but it disappeared near the town line. He couldn't tell which direction they went in.

He howled in pain.

She was gone! How could she be gone? How could he have let this happen? He was supposed to protect her!

"Elliott! What's wrong?" Tristan said, running up to him.

"She's gone! How could she be gone without a trace?" he cried.

"Elliott! What are you talking about?"

"Mia! She's gone! He took her!"

"What? That's not possible! I chased Dad all the way to the border of the next county. There's no way he could make it all the way back here and kidnap her," Tristan said, baffled.

"He had help, Tristan!" He whined and paced in a circle.

"Help? That's not like him."

"I smelled a vampire," Elliott spat. "They used something to mask their scent, and now I have no idea where she could be!" He growled.

"Working with vampires… that's even less like him. I thought he hated vampires."

"Apparently not more than he hates the idea of his children being with humans." He growled again and lay on the ground with a thump. "He warned me, Tris. He said I had until the end of winter, and I ignored it! I got too close and now… now he's ripped her away." He whimpered.

"Elliott… I'm so sorry." Tristan walked over and lay next to his brother to comfort him. "I will spend every moment I can looking for her. If you didn't feel your link to her break, then that means she's still alive out there. We'll find her, I promise."

CHAPTER TWENTY-TWO

ELLIOTT SAT ALONE IN Mia's dorm room, waiting for Thea to return from winter break. Every fiber of his being was telling him he shouldn't just be sitting there and he should be out scouring the woods from here to the edge of the ocean to find her. But Zeke insisted he be the one to tell Thea what happened, because she shouldn't have to hear it from some random cop.

Zeke had grown a soft spot for Thea over the past few months. He insisted they were just close friends who enjoyed gossiping about their best friends' relationship, but Elliott could tell he was falling for her. It would have been nice, seeing those two together and going on double dates with Mia. Now, it was nothing but a dream.

So, there he sat, hunched over around one of Mia's pillows, inhaling her scent to try to calm himself down. He closed his eyes and held the pillow close to his chest, pretending Mia was there with him. A tear slid down his cheek at the thought, knowing it wouldn't come true anytime soon.

He sat up and composed himself, wiping the tear off his face as he heard keys jiggling in the door.

"I hope you two aren't doing anything too bad 'cause I'm coming in anyway!" Thea yelled as she threw open the door. "I'm just kidding. I know you two are PG... only..." She paused when she noticed it was just Elliott sitting there. "Where's Mia?" she asked, looking around the room. "And why are you just sitting here with her pillow in your lap?"

"She... she's um..." He swallowed hard, a bubble of phlegm lodged in his throat from attempting not to cry.

Thea immediately picked up on his somber mood and dropped her bag on the floor, rushing over to him.

"Elliott?" She hopped up beside him on the bed. "Elliott, what's going on? Where is Mia?" she said nervously, placing her hand on his shoulder.

He turned his head to look at her. The tears pooling in his eyes were starting to overflow, and a look of concern crossed Thea's face.

"She's gone," he said, barely more than a whisper. He sniffled and wiped his eyes. "Kidnapped."

Her eyes grew wide, and she covered her mouth with her hands as she attempted to process what he had told her.

"I-I don't understand. How... I... W-What do you mean she was kidnapped?" she stuttered. "She can't be gone... she just can't! She's gotta be around here somewhere, right? Is that why all of those cop cars are outside? They're out looking for her?"

"They're trying to, yeah." He attempted to reassure her, but he doubted it sounded very convincing. If he couldn't even find her with his supernatural abilities, what chance did the police have?

"When..." Thea whispered. She swallowed hard, and Elliott could tell she was trying not to cry. "When did it happen? When was she taken?"

"Last night." He sniffled and turned away. "I was supposed to meet her here, but I was—I was running a bit late. I told her to wait until I was there before getting out, but you know how she is, she—she never listens." He let out a small chuckle, but it didn't sound right. "She got out and was getting her things when I heard a gasp and then... struggling before... before..." The words got caught in his throat and he sobbed again.

Thea leaned in and wrapped her arm around his shoulders.

"Hey, it's not your fault," she said softly, rubbing his back. "You couldn't have known."

Except it was his fault. If it wasn't for him, she would still be here right now, enjoying her time, probably laughing away with Thea. His father had warned him he would do something, and Elliott ignored him, thinking he had all the help in the world to protect her. Besides his father, he had no one to blame but himself.

"If I was just with her, I could've—"

"In moments like this..." She pulled away from their hug and looked him in the eyes. "I think it's best not to speculate on what could have happened and do what we can right now. Mia would want us looking for her, not blaming ourselves and wishing we'd done something different."

He looked back at her in astonishment at her unusually wise words. She wiped the tears from her eyes and turned to look out the window.

"I was supposed to come home early last night too, but I opted to stay one more night with my family," she said.

Elliott simply stared at her, unsure of what to say. Mia had never mentioned her coming home early. She must have been blaming herself as well, and here he was, being comforted by her instead.

"I could sit here and blame myself all day long for not being here for her," she continued. "Or I could go out there and help with the search for my best friend."

She turned back towards Elliott, who was awestruck by her sudden wisdom. Normally Thea was the lighthearted type who just went along with whatever came her way.

"With all of us looking, I'm sure we'll find her," she said, her voice wavering as if she almost didn't believe herself.

Elliott chuckled, wiping the tears from his eyes.

"Mia always says you were like a never-ending ball of positivity."

"I wouldn't say 'never-ending,'" she whispered, looking sadly back out the window again.

He frowned. He never meant to upset her by the statement. "No, of course not. I'm sorry."

"It's fine," she said, hopping off the bed. "You can make it up to me by finding Mia."

Her mood suddenly lightened again, though Elliott was hesitant to believe she was fully over the situation.

He nodded anyway and climbed off the bed. He grabbed his jacket off of Mia's desk chair and walked out the door with Thea, both of them ready to join the search.

Elliott pulled into his mother's driveway, eager to get to work looking for Mia with her and Lucy. His little sister was the best tracker he knew. If he had any chance of finding Mia, it was with her help.

He felt an eerie chill in the air as he stepped out of his car. Without a second thought, he rushed into his mother's home.

"Elliott!" His mother gasped as the front door slammed into the wall.

She stood in front of a hulking figure on the couch, looking nervously between the two of them. Lucy was at the top of the stares, glaring at the man as if she was mere seconds away from attempting to rip his throat out.

The scent of his father immediately smacked him in the face as the man stood up and turned towards him. His dark brown hair was slicked back, and he could see a new scar on his stubbly chin that wasn't there the last time Elliott saw him.

"Elliott, how nice of you to finally join us," his father said warmly, a fake smile plastered on his face.

"You bastard!" Elliott growled, lunging forward towards his father.

His fist hit the man's nose with a loud crunch, and they both fell backwards.

"Elliott!" his mother screamed, rushing to his side as he continued to wail on his father from on top of him.

"Fight back!" Elliott screamed. "You did this to her. Now fight back!"

"Elliott, stop it!" his mom screamed as she tried to pull him away from his father, but to no avail.

"If she dies, I swear to God I'm going to kill you!" He pulled his father up by his shirt to look him in the eyes, and a smug smile slipped across his face before Elliott punched him once again.

"Lucy, help me, please!" his mom begged.

She quickly ran down the stairs and helped to pull him away from his father. They held him back as he continued to growl.

"Elliott, calm down! You're not helping anyone by hurting him!" his mother yelled over him.

"And to think, I only came here to offer my assistance," his father said, cracking his nose back into place as his rapid healing took over. He stood up, and his face was covered in blood that was dripping down onto his black shirt.

"You liar," Lucy said angrily under her breath.

"Why would you want to help us?" his mother asked calmly.

"You're the reason she's gone!" Elliott yelled, attempting to lunge at him again. His mother and Lucy continued to hold him back from attacking.

"If you hadn't realized yet, she was taken by vampires, not me," he stated simply.

"Vampires who were working for you!" he screamed, finally shaking off his mother and Lucy's grip.

His father scoffed at the statement.

"Since when have I ever been involved with such arrogant creatures?"

"Probably since it would suit your own interests," his mother said, crossing her arms. "Just tell us where you've had her taken, Alastor. Enough of these games."

"We know it was you! You threatened her months ago, so don't even try to deny it!" Lucy said, placing her hands on her hips.

"This is none of your concern, half-breed," his father snapped.

"Don't you talk to her like that!" Elliott yelled. "Unless you want your face beaten in again."

"You really think you'd be able to do that to me again without me letting you?" He looked over at Elliott's mother. "You've done a terrible job at teaching these children manners." He sighed and ruffled his slicked-back hair. "Honestly, Gwen, none of this would've had to happen if you'd just left the boys with me."

Elliott and Lucy growled on their mother's behalf. She placed her arm out, and they instantly quieted.

"You do not get to come in here and berate me for how I raised my own children." She placed her hands on her hips and took a step towards him. "Because of you, our daughter felt she had to run away from us!"

Elliott took in a breath at the mention of his older sister. He could see the tears forming in her eyes at the thought of never finding her.

"Our eldest son has now refused to return to his human form, and you're about to drive your other son away too!" She was standing proudly in front of his father now, who had his arms crossed and an unreadable look on his face. "So I don't want to hear it from you whether or not I've failed our children, because as far as I'm concerned, you did that a long time ago!"

His father opened his mouth to speak, but in a moment that made Elliott glow with pride, she slapped him hard across the face.

"Unless the next words out of your mouth are where you've

had Mia taken, I suggest you leave," his mother hissed.

"You will never find her," his father growled at her, walking towards Elliott. "Unless, of course, you agree to never see her again and continue our family line the way it's supposed to be. Pure wolf."

"Never," he growled.

"Hm," his father hummed, a wicked smile spreading across his face. He turned and left the house without another word.

"We'll find her, Elliott," Lucy said, placing a comforting hand on his shoulder. He relaxed a bit at her touch.

"I know we will," he said, looking at her. "We have to."

CHAPTER TWENTY-THREE

MIA AWOKE IN A pitch-black room. She didn't remember going to sleep. In fact, she remembered little after she got back to the college. Did she pass out or something? And where was Elliott?

She got off the bed and stumbled through the dark, looking for the light switch. But she quickly realized this was not her dorm room she was in. When she finally hit the wall and found it, turning on the light, she gasped.

The room she was in was large, like a hotel suite. There was a four-poster bed on the back wall across from her, with a trunk lying at the foot of it. A flat screen TV was mounted on the wall next to her, with a small sofa in front of it for closer viewing.

A door was ajar on the left of the room, which looked like it led to a bathroom, while on the right there were windows covered in thick, luxurious black drapes.

Where on earth was she? And what happened to her? She rubbed her temples, begging her brain fog to go away so she could remember. When it didn't work, she ran over to the windows and threw open the curtains; the sun was just setting.

She recognized nothing outside. There was just a long, winding driveway surrounded by an enormous forest.

She tried to open the windows, but they were bolted shut. Why would they be bolted shut? She hyperventilated, clutching the charm of the necklace Elliott got her for comfort, when the handle on the door at the front of the room jiggled.

She stared in fear at the door, unsure of what was about to happen to her once it opened.

When it finally did, a small girl stepped in, her ebony skin striking against the brilliant white frilly dress she was in. Her hair was the color of the night sky and came to two neat little fluffy space buns at the top of her head. She reminded Mia of a doll with how sweet she looked, but there was something unsettling about her as well.

"Sorry about that," she said sweetly. "That darn key always gets stuck in the door to this room." She giggled, placing the key in a pocket of her dress.

When she looked up at Mia, her eyes darted from the window, then back up to her face.

"Oh, you won't get out that way." She giggled again. "It's been locked from the outside, and even if you did manage to get it open, it's quite the long fall. I doubt you'd survive if you jumped."

Mia continued to stare at her, dumbfounded. How was someone so chipper when speaking about death?

"I wasn't going to jump," Mia whispered.

"No, no, of course not!" She closed the door behind her and moved to the couch by the television.

She patted the seat next to her and looked at Mia expectantly.

When it was clear that Mia had no intention of moving from her spot by the window, the girl got up.

"I suppose we can talk standing too, if you feel more comfortable where you are," she said, flattening out her skirt and taking a step towards Mia.

Mia's heart started racing as she inched closer to her. She didn't know why she felt so afraid of such a small, innocent-looking girl, but every fiber of her being was telling her to run as far away as she could.

The girl stopped walking, as if in response to Mia's quickening heartbeat.

"You don't have to be afraid of me," she said, rubbing her arm nervously before looking back at Mia with big brown puppy-dog eyes. "I promise I'm not going to hurt you."

"You kidnapped me, and now you're telling me not to be afraid of you?" Mia spat.

"That is a very fair point... but! We didn't bring you here to hurt you. In fact, it's against our own moral code to hurt a human undeserving of it. So you can relax knowing you're safe and sound here with us!" she said, clapping her hands together with a smile.

"That doesn't make me feel better at all!" Mia shouted, tears stinging at the corners of her eyes. "Why am I here? What did I ever do to any of you? Just stop being so cryptic and tell me what's going on!"

"You didn't do anything to us..." She shook her head and sighed before deciding to continue. "In order to stay in this area, we had to make a deal with someone..." She looked away, unable to keep eye contact with Mia. "And you were the price."

Mia looked at her, dumbfounded. She was the price? What did that even mean?

"I-I don't understand. You're not making any sense!" Mia yelled.

The girl simply shrugged at her. "I'm not sure. We're all kinda in the dark on this one. Priscilla doesn't normally make deals, and this one is just so bizarre she's keeping the details to herself unless it's 'need to know.'"

"Need to know?"

"Yeah, like..." She took a second to think about it. "How you're not allowed to leave the property at all until..." She shifted uncomfortably and looked away from Mia.

"Until what?" Mia asked nervously.

"Until they say you can. And that all depends on how fast they can make some sort of other deal..."

"So it could be a few days or weeks..." Mia trailed off, her eyes stinging with tears she didn't want to fall.

"Or years..." the girl said quietly.

"Years..." Mia whispered, falling slowly down the wall until she was on the floor.

Her tears finally bubbled over, and she pulled her knees up, laying her head on them as she sobbed. Tears of grief for her lost life, tears of anger because she knew she didn't deserve this.

"There, there," the girl said, placing her arms around Mia in a hug.

Mia jumped at her sudden icy touch. She got there so quickly and quietly she wasn't even aware the girl had moved.

She attempted to shimmy out of her arms, but she just pulled her closer to her body.

"Shh, no, you stay right here and cry it out. It'll be all right; Dawn's here to help you through it," she said, stroking Mia's hair.

It reminded her of Elliott, and how he would stroke her hair mindlessly while they watched movies. She cried harder, knowing she would probably never see him again. He would probably move on without her, and she couldn't blame him for it.

She sat in Dawn's arms for what seemed like hours before her tears ran dry. What point was there in crying? It wouldn't fix anything. It wouldn't get her out of there.

"I've got to go now," Dawn said. "My mother will be in to talk to you soon, but feel free to take a look around."

Dawn stood up and helped Mia to her feet.

"I've loaded the wardrobe and dressers with lots of clothes for you, and you've got a bathroom attached here to the room. There's even a tub in there with jets for bubble baths!"

Mia nodded, barely paying attention to what she was saying.

Dawn walked over to the door, stopping in the open doorway. She turned back towards Mia.

"I do hope we can be good friends!" she said, smiling before shutting the door and leaving her alone in the room again.

Hoped they would be good friends? Mia laughed to herself and walked back over to the bed. She flopped down and curled herself into a ball.

Closing her eyes, she heard a sad howl from a wolf out in the distance. She continued to listen to it until she slowly drifted off into a dreamless sleep, hoping that when she awoke again, she would be back in her dorm to find out this was all just a horrible nightmare.

CHAPTER TWENTY-FOUR

MIA HEARD A LIGHT knocking at the door and hoped that when she opened her eyes, she would find herself back in her dorm room and it was just Thea at the door, saying she forgot her keys.

But when she did, her stomach dropped. She was still stuck in this room, alone, and who knows how far away from her friends and family.

She was on the verge of tears again when a young woman walked in. She had bright red hair tied in a French braid that hung over her shoulder, and just the sight of her sent a chill down Mia's spine.

She had a black lace top on with a white shawl wrapped around her shoulders, and a black pencil skirt completed the look. She stared at Mia with a bored look on her face as she approached her.

Mia sat up in bed and moved as far back as she could towards the headboard, her hand automatically grasping her necklace. This woman had a strange energy about her, and Mia did not want to be near her, but unlike Dawn, she didn't seem to care about Mia's discomfort.

She sat on the edge of the bed and stared at Mia for a moment before looking back at her nails, picking at the chipped polish.

"You have no reason to fear me, so back away from that headboard and relax," she said in an uninterested tone.

Mia looked her up and down before deciding to do what she said. If what Dawn told her was true, this woman wouldn't hurt her based on some sort of moral standard they had.

Was she the one Dawn called her mother? She looked only a few years older than her. How could that be possible?

"I suppose Dawn already explained your situation?" the woman said with a remorseful look.

Mia nodded slowly.

The woman looked away and sighed. "It is an unfortunate situation we have both been put in, and I am sorry that we had to do this to you," she said before turning back towards Mia with a serious look on her face. "But the family I have gathered here is special to me, and I will do anything to protect them. Even if that means taking orders from…" Mia could swear she heard a growl come out of her before she composed herself again and stood up, smoothing down her skirt. "Nevertheless, you will be staying with us until I get the word to release you. I have no need for a body to just be sitting here uselessly, so I have decided you will help around the house while you are here."

"E-Excuse me?" Mia chirped out, confused.

"This house is huge. We simply do not have the time to maintain it by ourselves, and if I have to have you here to fulfill our side of the agreement, then I might as well make you useful."

"Miss…" Mia stopped, realizing she had never gotten the woman's name. Dawn mentioned it quickly, but she just couldn't recall what it was.

"You may call me Priscilla, no 'miss' in front of it," she said with a sour look on her face. "That makes me sound so old."

"Priscilla…" She took a deep breath, closing her eyes and mustering up the courage to ask the questions that were plaguing her thoughts. "Who did this to me? Why am I here?"

Priscilla thought for a second before sitting back down on the edge of the bed, placing a motherly hand on Mia's leg for comfort. "Child, I know you must be very confused. The man who made this deal with us is someone we have had a problem with for years. I do not know why he wanted you out of the picture, and it is not my place to question him." She sighed and looked away, almost concerned.

So, this was just some random man that wanted her taken? That raised more questions than answers, which made her feel even more frustrated. She shifted uncomfortably on the bed.

Priscilla pressed her lips together in a line, clearly frustrated as well.

"I would very much like you to know that this kind of thing goes against everything I stand for. I do not enjoy taking free will from people," Priscilla said, leaning in close to Mia, looking directly into her eyes.

Mia leaned away from her as she saw Priscilla's eyes change to red. Her heart beat rapidly in her chest at the change. She tried to rub her own eyes, thinking she was seeing things, but Priscilla quickly pulled her arms back down to her sides.

"Calm down," she said, and Mia felt a wave of calm rush over her.

She blinked and shook her head at the strange feeling.

"Listen to me. You will not leave this property. You will not attempt to ask for help to escape this place. Do you understand?" Priscilla asked.

Mia nodded, unsure why she felt compelled to listen to her command.

Priscilla stood up, wiping down her skirt once again, and her eyes changed back to an emerald-green color.

"Take some time to compose yourself and then come downstairs. There are still two more family members you need to meet." She looked towards the window. "Do not take too long. The sun will be up soon."

Leaving it at that, Priscilla left the room, keeping the door wide open.

But what did she mean the sun was coming up soon? What did that have to do with meeting her family?

None of this made any sense. Between the mystery behind her kidnapping and now the weirdness of this family she found herself with, it left her head spinning.

She stared into the dark hallway outside of her room, unsure if she wanted to meet anyone else in this house.

She wasn't sure how long she had sat there before she finally found the courage to get up and walk through the doorway.

CHAPTER TWENTY-FIVE

MIA HESITANTLY MADE HER way out into the hallway, where she saw she was in a small mansion. The hall outside of her room opened up into a balcony overlooking the grand hall entranceway to the house.

The upper level arched around the entrance, with doors leading to what Mia suspected were the other bedrooms. Two enormous staircases faced across from the front door, leading upstairs.

Mia slowly crept down the hallway to her left and circled around to the first staircase leading down to the ground floor. The railings were dusty, and cobwebs lined the banister. It was no wonder they needed a maid.

She didn't know why she felt the need to be cautious around this house. Priscilla and Dawn made it quite clear that no one would hurt her here, and yet she still didn't feel safe.

Though she supposed being kidnapped should make her feel unsafe… Her mind was a mess right now, flitting between whether she should actually trust these people or trust her own intuition to run.

Once she made it to the ground floor, she looked towards the front doors, deciding if she should attempt to escape or not. What would they do if they caught her? Why would they leave her on her own like this, anyway? Maybe she was being watched?

She looked around the room, yet it seemed no one was there.

"Mia!" Dawn shouted.

Mia almost jumped out of her skin, turning around to see Dawn standing right behind her. When did she get there? She didn't even hear her walk in the room.

"Sorry, I didn't mean to scare you!" she said, jumping back and giving Mia puppy-dog eyes.

"Then why did you shout at me? Where did you even come from?" Mia said, looking around quickly.

She hugged herself nervously, trying to calm her racing heart.

"I thought you heard me come in," she said, looking disappointed. "I was in the kitchen and heard someone walking around out here." She suddenly perked up. "Are you hungry? We don't have a lot, but I'm sure we can find you something!"

She grabbed Mia's hand and dragged her through the doors behind them, through a large dining room, before rounding through a pair of double doors on the left and into an old-looking kitchen. The counters were bare, and it looked like it was hardly used. There was an island in the center of the room with nothing on it but dust.

Dawn heard her from all the way in here? She wasn't even aware she was making that much noise.

The window near the sink overlooked the back yard of the house, and she could see that the sun was coming up. Was that why no one was around? Priscilla did tell her to come down before the sun rose.

"You just missed the others. Katya said she was sick of waiting for you to come down, and Isaac is afraid of the sun, so they both went to bed," Dawn said. "I offered to stay up and wait for you, though. I love the sunrise, hence my name." She giggled. "I just have to stay out of the rays."

"Afraid of... the sun?" Mia asked. How could someone be afraid of the sun? "And what do you mean, they went to bed? Who goes to bed at sunrise?"

"Oh, did... did Priscilla not tell you?" she asked, cocking her head to the side, perplexed.

"Tell me what?"

"Oh... I don't know if I'm supposed to tell you or not if she didn't." She looked away and bit the nail of her thumb anxiously.

"Tell me what, Dawn? Nothing here makes sense!" She threw her arms up in frustration and began pacing the room. "You can't tell me why I've been taken. You can't tell me who ordered you to do it, and now you can't even answer my simple questions?" she shouted.

Dawn shuffled over and shushed her, looking frantically around the room.

"No! Answer my questions, please!" she begged, despite her heart beating loudly out of fear.

"Okay, okay! Just... quiet down. Katya is so not nice when you wake her from her beauty sleep."

Mia nodded. "Okay," she whispered.

"Well... you see... how do I put this?" Dawn hummed to herself. "We're vampires."

Mia stared at her a moment before she burst out laughing. "Vampires?" she choked out between laughs.

Dawn simply nodded, her face unreadable.

"You can't be serious," Mia said, catching her breath.

Dawn continued to stare at her awkwardly, unsure of how to respond to her laughter.

"All joking aside, though. Please answer my questions, Dawn," Mia said once she came down from her laughing fit.

She simply shrugged. "I'm not joking."

Mia was getting irritated. Why wouldn't she tell her the truth?

"Dawn, I'm serious."

"So am I."

They stood in silence while the sun slowly rose, lighting up the kitchen.

"Believe me or don't, but I promise you it's the truth," she said, dodging the light rays as she walked towards the door. "I've gotta go to bed, but feel free to raid the cabinets for some food."

Then Mia was left standing alone in the kitchen.

Why could no one around here give her any answers?

She walked over to the window and leaned on the counter, looking out into the back yard. There was a garden that was overgrown with weeds and various flowers. A small fountain stood in the center, with stone benches tipped over around it, but she could tell at one point it was probably very beautiful.

She suddenly realized just how utterly alone she was. Dawn told her they slept during the day, which, if she was telling the truth, meant that no one would be around right now.

She could attempt to escape... but something inside of her said that would be pointless. Still, she had to try.

She quietly made her way back to the foyer and looked around before creeping her way to the front door. She opened it slowly, flinching when it creaked momentarily.

Once she was on the front porch, she let out the breath she didn't realize she was holding. It lingered in the air of the chilly January morning. Her heart started beating faster as she wrapped her arms around herself and walked carefully down the steps and onto the driveway.

It was long and winding; she couldn't even see the road from the top. She didn't even know where she was, but someone was certain to help her if she could just make it to a town.

She took a deep breath, ready to run in case they saw her from their windows. She knew she wasn't fast, but if she was far enough away before they came after her, they couldn't possibly catch up before she found some help.

She took off, running as fast as she could down the driveway, breathing heavily since she wasn't used to sprinting like this. Halfway down the drive, she finally saw a large gate attached to the road.

"Almost there!" she panted to herself.

She could feel the phlegm getting stuck in her throat from running so hard when she suddenly came to a stop mere feet from the edge of the gate. She urged her feet to move, but they wouldn't budge.

She tried moving to the side, and that worked fine, but she couldn't go forward. She tried to yell for help, but nothing came out of her throat.

What was wrong with her?

She continued trying to step forward for ten minutes before giving up and sitting on the ground, tears stinging at the corners of her eyes. She was never getting out of here. Her own body wouldn't even let her move past the property line!

She looked up, remembering what Priscilla had told her in the bedroom. She wasn't allowed to leave the property or ask for help…

"There's no way…" she whispered to herself, looking back at the house.

She tried to think of any other possible explanation for why she was following Priscilla's words to a tee. Anything else besides vampires—that kind of thing couldn't possibly exist.

Maybe she was hypnotized somehow… that kind of thing could happen in real life. But then again, she saw Priscilla's eyes change color. Was it possible that wasn't a trick of her mind?

She shook her head, trying to ignore that idea.

After about an hour of sitting there in the cold, no cars had driven by. She couldn't even hear anyone around, which meant she was most likely in the middle of nowhere.

She sighed and started her long trek back to the house, shuffling her feet and taking her time before she finally made it back up to the porch. She turned around to look at the view; the house wasn't exactly on a hill, but she could still tell there wasn't much around the area. Just a dense forest surrounding the entire property and beyond.

She went back inside, and her stomach grumbled at her as soon as she shut the front door.

"Have a pleasant run, did you?" Priscilla's voice rang from above her.

Looking up, Mia saw she was sitting on the railing of the second floor between the two staircases.

"Why… why couldn't I leave?" Mia muttered out.

"Because I said you could not." She rolled her eyes. "Dawn told me you did not believe her when she told you we were vampires."

She jumped off the banister and landed gracefully on the first floor without a single injury. Mia gaped at her as she suddenly appeared in front of her face at lightning speed.

"Do you believe her now?" she said tauntingly.

Mia backed away from her slowly and hit the front door.

"I told you already, you have nothing to fear from us," she said calmly, not moving an inch towards Mia. "We may not harm you, and even if we could, I have drilled it into this family that we do not harm humans unless under extreme circumstances."

"B-But… you… don't you drink…" Mia gulped, unable to complete her sentence, fear coursing through every bone in her body.

Priscilla rolled her eyes. "Blood. Yes, we do. But we try to keep it to blood bags only, and if we need it fresh, there are plenty of evil beings out there that deserve to be scared out of their wits." She let a grin slip across her face. "We never kill people unless it is truly necessary. It causes too many issues."

"Is that… is that true for all vampires?"

"For most, but there are some you should never cross." She looked away, almost shamefully. "As for you, I have no intention of adding you as a member of my family, so you need not worry about such things. Just go about your business here, and I am sure we will get the word to release you before you know it."

She smiled sadly at Mia before turning away and walking towards the steps, stopping at the bottom before speaking again.

"And Mia, do get yourself some food from the kitchen. I could hear your stomach rumbling from upstairs."

Mia nodded without looking at her. She walked like a zombie towards the kitchen to check for whatever scraps they might have lying around for a human to eat. Her brain felt foggy with the realization that this was all happening.

Vampires were real. And if they were real... what else was?

CHAPTER TWENTY-SIX

AFTER SHE HAD EATEN, Mia went back up to her room and hid under the covers of the bed, trying desperately to wrap her mind around this new world she found herself in.

At some point, she drifted off to sleep, only to be awoken by a soft shaking of her shoulders.

"Mia," Dawn's kind voice sang through her ears. "Mia, it's time to wake up."

"Hm?" Mia groaned, rolling over onto her back and slowly opening her eyes.

"There she is," Dawn said with a smile.

Mia simply frowned at her, reminded again of how trapped she was in this place.

"It's time to get up and meet the rest of the family!" she said cheerily, not quite catching on to Mia's annoyed mood.

"What time is it?" Mia asked, sitting up.

"Almost midnight. We weren't sure when you went to bed, so we wanted to make sure you got a decent amount of sleep before you had to start work."

"Midnight?" she asked, rubbing her eyes before remembering what they were. "Oh, right… vampires."

"So, you do finally believe me! I knew you'd come around," she said, pulling Mia into a quick hug that she didn't appreciate.

"Priscilla didn't tell you about this morning?" Mia said when she was finally released from Dawn's grasp.

"Tell me what?" She cocked her head to the side.

"I guess she didn't find it too important if she didn't mention it to you."

"She's very secretive sometimes, but once you get to know her, you'll like her!"

"Yeah… I don't think so," Mia said, rolling off the bed and standing up.

"Where are you going?"

"To 'meet the family' like you've been begging me to since last night," Mia said, not holding back the annoyance in her voice.

"Not like that, you're not!" Dawn said, hopping up off the bed and placing her hands on her hips. "You need a shower and a change of clothes!"

Dawn pushed her into the bathroom, closing the door and locking Mia in by herself before she could even understand what was happening.

"I'll pick something nice out for you while you're in there!" she said through the door.

Mia sighed and turned around. The bathroom itself was just as luxurious as the rest of the house. It had an enormous bathtub on one side, just like Dawn had mentioned, and right across from it was a spacious shower with beautiful sliding glass doors accented with a frosted floral design on them.

She turned the shower on and quickly stripped her clothes. She had meant to shower earlier when she had finished eating, but once she got back up to her room, she sat on her bed and didn't want to get up again.

Trying to process everything she was feeling just made her feel even worse, and being completely alone didn't help either. The longer she was there, the larger the hole in her chest felt.

She longed for her friends and family, but most of all, Elliott. He had to be frantic hearing her kidnapping over the phone. She wished she had listened to him and just stayed in the car like he asked her to.

She sobbed again, falling to her knees and curling into a ball on the shower floor. The hot water raining down on her was only a little comforting as she cried.

When she felt like she had run out of tears, she finally stood up again.

After washing her hair and a quick scrub of some soap and body wash, she turned off the shower and slid the glass doors open. She wrapped a towel around her hair and another around her body before cracking open the bathroom door to see that Dawn had left some clothes on the floor.

Dawn had picked her out a black long sleeve shirt that fell casually off of her shoulder, and a pair of leggings with a fun purple zig-zag print on them.

She brushed her hair and left it down for once, falling in messy waves down her back, before finally leaving the bathroom.

Dawn was sitting on her bed, flicking through a book, and she looked up when Mia walked in.

"Took you long enough!" she said, shutting the book and hopping off the bed.

Mia was glad she didn't mention hearing her crying. Even over the sound of the water running, she was sure Dawn could hear it.

Dawn walked over to Mia and stood in front of her with her hands on her hips. "Man, did I do a good job with that outfit or what?" she said proudly.

"I'm gonna go with 'or what,'" Mia said harshly, causing Dawn to frown.

"It's not my fault you have so much of a laid-back style that there's not much to work with," she said, crossing her arms defensively. "Now come on. I'm sure Katya's waiting to go out, so we should probably introduce you before she gets angry."

Dawn grabbed Mia's arms and led her back downstairs.

Instead of heading straight back into the kitchen, they took a right turn through a pair of doors and into what looked like a living room.

There were three couches facing a giant flat screen TV mounted onto the wall above an enormous entertainment system. Along the walls were bookshelves filled to the brim with more books than anyone could possibly read.

Sitting on the couch facing them was a boy who looked to be around twenty. He was a bit on the scrawny side, with dark brown hair pulled up into a bun. He was watching something on the television but popped right out of his seat when he noticed the two of them walk in.

"You must be Mia!" he said, a slight Spanish accent bleeding through as he spoke, reminding her of Erika. He walked over and shook her hand, a bright smile on his face. "It's great to finally meet you."

Mia nodded at him with a confused look on her face as he shook her hand.

"This is Isaac. He's the newest addition to our little family here. But no worries—his hunger is completely under control!" Dawn said, reminding Mia exactly why she should be worried.

"Oh yeah, after a few years, I think I got the hang of this vampire thing!" He laughed.

"Right..." Mia said nervously.

Dawn looked around the room with a confused look on her face. "Where's Katya?" she asked Isaac.

"She went to her room to get changed." He paused and listened for a moment. "It sounds like she's on her way back down, though."

He gestured for them to make their way back into the foyer. As they walked through the double doors out of the living room,

Mia saw a gorgeous girl with blonde hair coming down the steps.

She caught a sense of déjà vu as she saw this girl in her red leather jacket with the fur collar. After a moment, it struck her, the memory of her kidnapping flashing back through her mind.

"You," she breathed out, no more than a whisper.

Dawn and Isaac looked at her, confused.

"Oh, good, you're finally awake," she said with the slightest Russian accent as she came to a stop in front of Mia, Dawn, and Isaac. "I'm Katya, you're Mia. Good, glad we had this little meeting, so you can tell Priscilla it happened. Now I'm off." She made her way around them, heading for the front door.

"Wait, that's it?" Dawn said, chasing after her.

"What do you mean 'that's it'? I met her, didn't I?" she asked, stopping with her hand on the doorknob.

"Well, yeah, I guess, but—"

"Then we're done here. I'll see you all later!" She waved at them and walked out the door.

"That's our Katya," Isaac said, shaking his head.

"Is she always that…" Mia searched for a good word to describe her.

"Friendly?" Isaac said sarcastically. "Yeah. But you learn to live with it."

"Oh, come on, she's not all bad!" Dawn said, skipping back over to them. "She's probably just moody because she's late meeting her girlfriend."

"Well, look who has finally joined us," Priscilla said, coming out of the dining room. "I assume you are all acquainted now?"

"Yes, ma'am!" Dawn said cheerily, giving Priscilla a big smile.

"Good, good. Listen, I have to go out for a bit to replenish our blood supply. So I am going to need you two to walk Mia through her day-to-day chores and what her new sleep schedule will be like. Can you do that for me?" she said, flashing Dawn a big smile back as she leaned down and placed a hand on her shoulder.

"Of course, Miss Priscilla," Isaac said.

"Oh, Isaac, what have I said about calling me 'miss'?" she asked like a disappointed parent.

"Right, sorry," he said nervously, scratching the back of his head.

Mia couldn't help but notice how friendly they were to each other, the way Dawn looked at Priscilla like she was her entire world. It made Mia ache for her own family back home.

Dawn suddenly wrapped her arm around Mia's. "We'll be sure to take good care of her!"

"That is what I like to hear," Priscilla said, leaning back up and looking around the room. "Did Katya already leave?"

"In her usual dramatic fashion," Isaac said.

"All right. Well then, I will be back as soon as I can."

She kissed them both on the cheek before walking out the door.

"Well then, where should we start?" Dawn asked.

CHAPTER TWENTY-SEVEN

AWN AND ISAAC HAD given Mia a tour of the entire house, along with a rundown of what they expected of her. She was to be nothing more than a mere maid to them, and Priscilla wasn't joking about the house needing some work done. It looked like no one had ever bothered to even try to dust the place.

There were spiderwebs hanging off most of the banisters, and the windows were so dirty you could barely see out of them. Not to mention the crumbs in the living room that looked like it hadn't been vacuumed in ages, and Mia didn't even know vampires ate regular food. She assumed the snacks she found in the pantry earlier were there because they knew she would need food but didn't know what to get.

"And that would be it for the inside of the house," Isaac said as they finished up the tour back in the foyer.

"The inside? You mean there's more outside?" Mia said, shocked.

"Don't tell me you didn't see the garden yet?" Dawn said. "It's the loveliest part of the whole place!" She grabbed Mia's hand and led her towards the back of the house with more strength than a girl her size should have.

"From what I saw from the kitchen window, it looked pretty dead," Mia said.

"Well, yeah, the flowers are dead, but the vines are still growing, and the possibilities of this place are magical!" Dawn said as she pulled her through the back door in the kitchen and out into the gardens.

Dawn let go of Mia's hand as she ran out into the unkept garden. Weeds sprouted out between the cobblestone path that led to a broken fountain with dirty stone benches tipped over around it. The stone flowerpots littered throughout the garden held decayed flowers, and overgrown vines and weeds surrounded the whole thing. Everything was coated in a light dusting of snow from earlier that day.

The only thing that didn't look completely destroyed or decayed was the tiny shed toward the right of the yard.

Dawn twirled around as she soaked in the moonlight.

"She's a bit of a dreamer," Isaac said, casually walking up beside her as she continued to watch Dawn dance around the dead garden.

"I can... see that," Mia said hesitantly.

"Come on, Mia, there's so much to see!" she yelled, waving her over.

Isaac flipped a switch beside the door, and a lamp flickered on, barely flooding the grounds with enough light for Mia to see where she was walking.

Impatiently, Dawn ran over and grabbed Mia's hands again. Dragging her over to one of the toppled-over benches, she picked it up with ease and set it back into place.

She wiped the dirt off of it and sat down, patting the spot next to her for Mia to sit. Isaac casually made his way over and sat across from them on the edge of the fountain.

"Isn't it just wonderful back here?" she asked, staring around as Mia sat down.

"It's... something... I guess."

"Oh, come on! Just think of all the possibilities! You could really make this place shine, I know it!"

"Me?" Mia looked at her like she had two heads. She knew at this point she was required to clean the house, but being a landscaper was an entirely different ordeal.

"Yeah! We're letting you do whatever you want to the garden! It got pretty overgrown in the years we weren't here, and Priscilla says it's pretty pointless to fix it up." She looked up at the sky sadly. "But you can do whatever you want with it in your spare time. Maybe it'll be a nice distraction for you while you're here." She turned her head back towards Mia and smiled sadly.

Mia simply stared back at her, not sure what to say. She had no desire to renovate this garden. She didn't need a distraction. What she needed was to leave.

"You don't want to, do you?" Dawn said, barely a whisper. Yet she didn't try to hide the disappointment in her voice.

"Dawn, don't guilt the poor girl. She hasn't even been here for two days. Give her some time," Isaac said, getting up and walking to stand in front of Dawn.

"But she can be happy here, right?" she asked him, completely ignoring the fact that Mia was sitting right next to her.

"Maybe she will be, maybe she won't. Not everyone sees the world from your perspective," Isaac said, leaning down and kissing Dawn on the forehead. "Why don't you go get us something to drink? I'm sure Mia here could probably use something to warm her up."

"Oh no! Is it really that chilly out?" Dawn said, popping up off the bench. "I'm sorry, Mia, I wasn't thinking. I'll go get you some tea!" She turned to walk away before stopping and looking back at Mia quizzically. "Or would you prefer hot chocolate?"

"Hot chocolate is fine, thanks." Mia chuckled at her strange behavior.

"Hot cocoa it is, then!" she said, rushing off back into the house.

Isaac sat down next to her, and she could tell he was as uncomfortable around her as she was with him.

"I'm sorry about Dawn. She hasn't really spent a lot of time around other people, so she's a little... out there," he said, staring down at the stones.

"It's fine..." Mia said, not sure how to speak with him. He seemed very introverted compared to Dawn, and awkward with conversation. "Why hasn't she been around people?"

"Well..." He bit his lower lip, thinking. "You see, Priscilla found her when she was a baby. This was maybe back in the late 1800s, early 1900s, I think..." He stared off into the fountain, trying to remember. "I never really got all the details, but from what she told me, she was found in her mother's arms on the brink of death. Her mom was already long gone, looked like she'd been through something rough, but Priscilla, being who she is, took her in and looked after her until she was old enough to decide if she wanted to stay human or become a vampire."

"Clearly, she chose the latter."

"Yeah. But because Priscilla was so overprotective of her, she kind of lived a sheltered life."

"Isaac! What are you telling her about me?" Dawn ran back over, three mugs in hand.

"Not much, just all the family secrets." He shrugged.

"Isaac!" she yelled like a child throwing a tantrum, stomping her feet quickly on the ground.

"I'm joking! I'm joking!" He laughed, getting up and grabbing the mugs out of her hands.

He handed one to Mia, and she didn't realize how cold she was until the warmth of the mug touched her skin. She sat there for a moment, just letting her hands melt a bit before taking a sip.

Dawn sat back down next to Mia and, after taking a long sip from her mug, leaned in towards her. "So, what did he really tell you?" she whispered.

"I'm right here, you know," he said.

"Not much really," Mia said, sipping her hot chocolate again. "You mentioned Priscilla taking Dawn in because that's just the way she is. What did you mean by that?"

"You told her about Priscilla finding me as a baby?" Dawn said, shocked.

"Only the cliff notes version." Isaac shrugged. "And I know she may not seem it, but Priscilla is actually a kind woman. She took each of us in when we were in an awful place and treated us better than we'd ever had in our human lives. Accepted us for who we were, no questions asked." He looked down at the ground and smiled.

"Yeah, she's the best!" Dawn suddenly jumped up and grabbed Mia's hands around the mug. "I promise you, Mia, you'll feel like family in no time! It'll be like one long sleepover. You won't even want to go home anymore!"

Isaac sighed, and being reminded of home caused Mia to tear up again.

"I think it's time we go inside," he said.

Mia nodded and followed him, going straight up to her room, hiding under the covers, and falling asleep.

Mia awoke around noon, the midday sun streaming in through the windows. She groaned and rolled out of bed, making her way to the bathroom. Looking in the mirror, she realized she had never actually changed clothes before going to bed.

She rummaged through the drawers of the two dressers they had put in her room before finding something suitable to wear. Quickly changing into a purple sweatshirt and jeans, she tied her hair into two low pigtails before she went downstairs to the kitchen to find something to eat.

Walking in, she saw the mugs from last night sitting in the sink, unwashed.

Mia sighed. "So it begins."

She picked them up and started scrubbing them, relieved to find that Dawn and Isaac were actually drinking hot chocolate and not blood, when she saw the clumps of chocolate powder stuck to the bottom of the cup.

After she had eaten, she got to work on the rest of the house, starting with the dusting in the foyer. She had gotten through almost the whole first floor in a few hours before stopping in the kitchen for a break.

The sun would be going down soon, and she would have Dawn breathing down her neck again. Leaning on the counter, she looked out at the overgrown mess of a garden in the back yard.

Maybe when spring came around and it was warm enough, she could do something with it after all...

CHAPTER TWENTY-EIGHT

SIX MONTHS. IT HAD been six whole months since Mia had disappeared, with still no leads on where they had taken her.

His father had returned at least once every month with his offer to release Mia in exchange for Elliott's own future, but he couldn't give in to him. There had to be another way to find her, and he wasn't going to stop looking until he did.

He had combed the entire forest multiple times, searching for Mia, but to no avail. Vampires tended to keep to themselves and were excellent at hiding. She could be anywhere by now.

"Still at it?" Lucy said, trotting up to Elliott.

"I'm never going to stop looking for her—you know that, Lucy," he said, sniffing the air again for any trace of her scent.

"I know." She looked down, whining. "But even I couldn't pick up her scent, Elliott. Wherever she is, it's far away from here."

Lucy was the best tracker in their whole family. If she couldn't sniff her out, then finding Mia seemed like a long shot.

"Then I'll leave, spread my search out farther," he said, looking deep into the trees of the forest.

Lucy quickly looked at him, surprised.

"What about school?"

"I don't care about that anymore!" he snapped at her.

Lucy recoiled and backed away from him, whimpering.

"I'm sorry, Lu," he said sadly, walking over to comfort her. "I just—I've got to find her. I'll run the entire country if I have to."

"Oh yeah? And what about Mom? Or Zeke? Or me?" she yelled, backing away from him. "I know it hurts that Mia's disappeared, but that doesn't mean you can ignore the rest of your friends and family!"

"I'm not ignoring anyone," he growled.

"Zeke says he barely sees you! That you're out here all day long now that classes are over, and you don't come home until the middle of the night when you know he'd be out somewhere."

"Since when are you and Zeke such good friends?"

"Since you stopped being his!" she shouted. "He can't talk to you apparently, so he sees what he can learn from me, which honestly isn't a lot, considering you'd rather be by yourself nowadays."

Elliott whined, lying down with his head on his paws.

"Oh, don't you whine at me just because you've made poor decisions. You think you're the only one hurting, Elliott? She was going to be my sister someday!" She growled, trotting up to stand in front of him. "And Thea, poor Thea, she lost her best friend and has no idea why. Not to mention her parents. Have you even spoken to them since the searches stopped being as frequent? It's been six months, Elliott. It's time to stop being so dramatic and let others in. Let us help you grieve." She lay next to him.

He looked away from her, and she sighed.

"At least let us help you look for her. I know Tristan's out chasing your dad in hopes of him leading him to her, but maybe Zeke could use his vampire connections to find something out. Or we could get that witch in town to use a tracking spell or something. You're not alone. I don't know how many times we have to remind you of that."

The two sat in silence for a few minutes. She was right, of course. Every time it came to Mia, he lost his common sense. He made so much progress with his family once he finally let her be a part of his life, and now that she was gone, he reverted right back to square one.

"When did you get to be so wise?" he asked.

"About the same time you got so dumb." She laughed, and he nipped at her ear. She bit back at him.

"Seriously, I'm the big brother. I'm supposed to be the one giving advice."

"Well, not anymore! Go home and get some sleep. You look like shit."

"Gee, thanks," he said sarcastically.

"Well, it's the truth! And as your sister, I'm obligated to tell it as it is."

She got up and started walking back the way she came.

"Lucy, wait!" he yelled, falling in line beside her. "You think I could go back with you? I'm not quite ready to deal with Zeke yet."

"Yeah, sure," she said, bumping his side as they walked. "I'm sure Mom would love to see you, anyway."

Elliott let out a deep breath, trying to calm himself before he entered his apartment. It seemed silly that he was nervous about talking to Zeke again, but he'd been avoiding him for months now, and he just wasn't sure how he would react.

Finally, he opened the door and walked inside. Zeke was lying on the couch as usual, watching some reality show on the television.

"I was wondering how long you were going to stand out there," he said without moving.

"Hey, man…" Elliott said nervously.

"Hey? You've been ignoring me for months, and all I get is a 'hey'?" he said, sitting up and turning towards Elliott.

Zeke stared at him for a moment, taking in his disheveled look. His hair was a mess, and his clothes were covered in dirt from being shoved in a tree stump. His eyes were carrying bags underneath them from his lack of sleep, and he smelled like he was in desperate need of a shower.

"Dude, you look like shit," Zeke said.

"Yeah, I know," Elliott said as he finally walked into the room and sat next to Zeke on the couch. "Listen, Zeke, I'm sorry for being so absent lately. It's just…"

"The Mia thing. I know." He looked down sadly.

"It's not just that," Elliott said.

Zeke gave him a confused look.

"What else is it, then?" Zeke asked.

"It's… well… You and Thea—"

"You're jealous of me and Thea? That's why you've been avoiding me?" Zeke cut in. His eyes glowed red out of anger.

"No, nothing like that!" Elliott said. "She just… she reminds me of her. I can still sort of smell Mia's scent when she's around."

"Shit, man, I'm sorry. I didn't even think of that," Zeke said, concern in his voice. "She said she carries around a couple of these crystals Mia got awhile back. It didn't even cross my mind that the bag would still smell like her."

He sighed. "I can't blame her for wanting to keep a piece of Mia with her." He looked at Zeke in confusion. "But why would Mia need crystals? She's not a witch."

"Thea said they picked them up a couple months ago after coming across that wiccan store in town. To help with her writer's block or something."

Elliott nodded at him absentmindedly when a thought crossed his mind.

"Speaking of that wiccan store—"

"I already tried to ask her," Zeke said, not letting him finish his question.

"You did?" Elliott asked, surprised.

"Yeah, it's not like I haven't also been trying to find Mia in my free time." Zeke shrugged.

"So, what did she say?" Elliott asked eagerly.

"She said she already tried, but something was blocking her tracking spell. Your father really pulled out all the stops for this one."

"Damn." He breathed out.

Elliott bit his lip, thinking. *There goes one lead.*

"And you're sure you don't have any vampire contacts you could ask?"

"It's not like we all keep tabs on each other," he said, offended, as he sat back on the couch. "Besides, most of us are keeping to the shadows these days, since those disappearances have started happening."

Elliott sighed. "Well, it was worth a shot."

"Hey," Zeke said, placing a hand on Elliott's shoulder. "It's only a matter of time before they slip up. We'll get her back."

Elliott nodded at him and turned his head towards the TV. "I just hope she's okay when we do."

CHAPTER TWENTY-NINE

MIA COULDN'T BELIEVE SIX months had already gone by. It was fast, but not fast enough. She wished every day that it would be her last in this house, but of course that wish never came true.

She'd gotten into the rhythm of staying up until three in the morning and then sleeping in until one in the afternoon before doing her chores. With her constantly cleaning the house, it actually looked presentable again. She hated to admit it, but she was kind of proud of the work she'd done here.

Once the weather got warmer, she had begun picking up and cleaning the garden. Dawn was excited to see what the outcome was going to be once Mia told her it was ready. For some reason she wanted it to be a surprise and stayed away from the back yard, which meant Isaac had to help with any heavy lifting.

Mia wiped the sweat off her forehead as she hung the last of the string lights Dawn picked up for her across the garden. They stretched from the house to the back shed, and she was excited to see what they'd look like in the dark.

She sat down on the ladder and looked around at what she'd created. It had taken her about four straight months of work, but it was worth it. The dead flowers were gone, and in their place were some fake ones that looked as realistic as plastic flowers could be. The weeds were all gone, and the cobblestone path was scrubbed clean of dirt and debris. She cut the vines back, so they only wrapped stylishly around the legs of the benches or trees and portions of the house and fountain.

The place finally looked alive. And tonight, she'd show it to Dawn.

The project was a delightful distraction from her predicament, and she was afraid of what would happen now that it was complete.

She quickly set to work putting the gardening equipment away before heading inside. Looking at the clock, it was only six, two more hours until the sun went down.

She groaned and headed upstairs to shower before making food for herself. That killed about an hour, so she got to work on cleaning the kitchen from top to bottom just as the sun started to set.

The sun had gone down for about an hour and a half before Mia went in search of Dawn. Usually Dawn would find her, not the other way around, but she was getting eager to show off her work on the back yard.

As she walked through the dining room and into the foyer, the house was eerily silent. Usually there was at least some noise, whether it be Katya on the phone with her girlfriend, or Isaac watching something on the television. But today there was just... nothing.

Making her way upstairs, she saw Isaac, Dawn, and Katya leaving Priscilla's room at the end of the hallway. Dawn and Isaac looked nervously in her direction, while Katya just walked by her, a neutral expression on her face, before she turned and walked into her room.

She never spent time with Katya to get to know her like she did with Dawn and Isaac, but being around her made Mia nervous. She wasn't sure if Katya hated her being here or just didn't care for her at all.

"Hey... is everything okay?" Mia asked curiously as she approached Dawn and Isaac.

They kept looking at each other, and then back at Mia.

"That would depend on your definition of okay," Dawn said.

Isaac elbowed her in the side, and she let out a small yelp of pain in response.

"It's nothing you need to be worried about," Isaac said.

Mia found that hard to believe given their demeanors on the subject, but if they didn't want to talk about it, then there was no use trying to get the information out of them.

"So, was there something you needed?" Isaac said when she hadn't spoken after a while.

"Oh, yeah! I finished up the garden today," Mia said, and Dawn's eyes lit up with joy.

"You did?" she asked excitedly.

"Yeah, that's why I was looking for you. I wanted you to be the first to see it," she said with a smile.

"Oh! You're the best, Mia!" Dawn giggled, giving her the biggest hug. Once she let go, she grabbed Mia's hand. "Let's go!"

They barely made it a few feet down the hall before Dawn stopped and turned around. Isaac had his hand on her shoulder and was shaking his head. Dawn's spark immediately diminished.

"Just for a minute?" Dawn begged.

"You heard the rules; no going out tonight, Dawn," Isaac said.

"Rules? What are you two talking about?" Mia asked.

"Nothing, don't worry about it," Isaac said.

Dawn looked down at her feet sadly, refusing to look Mia in the eyes.

"You're telling me not to worry about it, yet the both of you look like you've seen a ghost!" Mia said, placing her hands on her hips.

"It sure feels like it…" Dawn mumbled, causing Isaac to elbow her again.

"Wait, is it a ghost? I suppose if vampires exist, it would make sense for ghosts to as well," Mia said distractedly.

Isaac rubbed his temples as if the conversation was giving him a headache.

"It's not a ghost, and yes, they do exist. But that's not the point!" Isaac said, growing more annoyed by the minute.

"Ugh, can you three just shut up already?" Katya interrupted, stepping out of her room.

Mia hadn't even noticed they stopped in front of her door. A chill went down her spine at seeing her so angry.

"Sorry, Kat, we didn't mean to be so loud," Dawn said, giving her biggest puppy-dog eyes.

Katya sighed. She looked Mia in the eyes as hers began to glow a bright red. "Just finish up your chores for the night, and when you're finished, go back to your room and stay there." Mia caught on quickly that glowing eyes meant vampire powers, which also meant this was another order she couldn't refuse. "And don't you dare go outside tonight. Understand?" she spat.

Mia nodded before turning on her heels and heading back down the stairs to grab the cleaning supplies. She couldn't even control her own movements, her brain in a fog from the compulsion. She barely heard their conversation as she left.

"Why'd you go and do that, Kat?" Dawn whined at her.

"Because you wouldn't, and she needed to leave," Katya said.

"You know it's mean to take away people's free will!" Dawn said.

"Dawn, come on, it happened and there's nothing we can do about it. Let's just go find something to do," Isaac said.

"I'm sorry it had to be this way, Dawn, but that's just how things go sometimes…" Katya said, her voice fading away, and Mia made her way into the dining room to dust the china.

She went through the rest of the night doing her chores in a daze, seeing no one else in the house before finally heading upstairs to her room. Once the door was shut, her mind finally snapped back to her own.

Her head was pounding as she made her way to the bathroom and grabbed some pain relief pills from the medicine cabinet. After taking them, she made her way back to her bed and pulled the journal Dawn got her from the drawer of her bedside table.

Over the past six months, she had kept notes on the family and anything they told her about their lives. It seemed like the secret they were keeping had to do with their past. Maybe she could find the answers in one of the stories Dawn had told her.

Skimming through her notes, she didn't seem to find anything that would leave them all as upset as they seemed to be. She wanted to brainstorm some explanations, but her headache was only getting worse.

She groaned, rolling over in her bed and throwing the journal back in the drawer. She wasn't going to get answers anytime soon, but she was used to it by now. With this family, it seemed like everything was a secret.

All she could do for now was shut off her light and sleep.

CHAPTER THIRTY

Mia spent her day reading in the garden, feeling utterly alone once again. She figured someone might as well use the space since she put so much effort into cleaning it up. As the sun descended behind the tree line, she decided to go back inside, as it was getting too dark to read.

She hoped things would be back to normal tonight, or as normal as things could be with what her life was like now. As overwhelming as Dawn was to be around, she had to admit she missed her presence last night. It was lonely having no one to talk to as she was forced to do her work around the house.

She made her way through the dining room and up the stairs, only to find Priscilla waiting for her outside her door.

"Ah, there you are," Priscilla said. "I have to speak with you about something."

She opened Mia's door and gestured for her to go inside. Priscilla followed her in, and the two of them sat on the sofa opposite each other. Mia looked at her nervously. She hadn't had a one-on-one with Priscilla since her first night there. Could this be about last night? Was she actually going to get answers about what was going on?

"By now you have probably noticed we are all a bit on edge at the moment," Priscilla stated.

"Yeah, it's, uh… pretty hard to miss." Mia chuckled nervously.

"Yes, well, that is what I am here to discuss with you. I do not need your curiosity running rampant and getting you into trouble."

"So what is it, then?" she asked.

"We have heard through the grapevine that there is someone dangerous in the area, and that he might attempt to come here," she said seriously.

"Dangerous?" Mia laughed. "You're vampires! What could be so dangerous that you'd be so scared?"

Priscilla sat in silence, her face never losing the serious look from the start of the conversation.

"A lot of things, actually, but hopefully you will never have to meet any of them."

"So then… who is this guy that's got you all so spooked?"

Priscilla looked away, suddenly unable to make eye contact. That was intriguing to Mia. Whoever this person was, he clearly had something to do with Priscilla's past.

"That is none of your concern."

"Then why even tell me about him?" Mia crossed her arms and leaned back on the sofa.

"So that you can understand my reasoning behind what I am about to do."

"What are you about to do?" Mia asked, confused.

Her heart raced, unsure of Priscilla's intentions.

Priscilla sighed, and she seemed to be conflicted about her decision.

"From now until this threat is gone, you are not to leave this room, not even during the day. We will bring you food and anything else you need, but we do not need him catching a whiff of a human here and coming after you."

"What? You cannot be serious!" Mia shouted, standing up.

"I can assure you I am completely serious," Priscilla said, standing up and pushing Mia back down into her seat.

Mia crossed her arms defiantly. "So then, I really am a prisoner now."

Priscilla rolled her eyes. "Oh, do not be so dramatic. It is just until he skips town again, so it should not be that long. It is for your own protection."

"Fine. But I still think it's cruel," Mia said with a huff.

"I am not a fan of it either, but it is the best I can do," she said, standing up.

"You could let me go back to my family. I was safe there," Mia joked. If only it were that simple.

"Nice try, but I will not give up my family just because of a minor threat like—" She paused, catching herself before she said too much. She sighed again, turning back to Mia. "Please do not give me a reason to compel you to stay in this room. I do not enjoy taking away someone's free will. However, I will not hesitate to, if it is for your own good."

She turned around and left the room, leaving Mia sitting on the sofa alone once again.

"So much for getting answers." Mia groaned, leaning back into the pillows.

As usual, she got more questions than answers. And even worse? Now she was stuck in this room.

She pushed herself off the sofa and walked over to her bedside table, pulling her journal out and sitting on the bed. Priscilla was hiding something about this "dangerous person." There was something personal about it, and she was going to find out what it was.

She flipped to the back of the notebook, where she kept her notes on the family. She'd been trying to piece together their whole story since she'd gotten here, but there wasn't a lot to go on.

According to her notes, Priscilla had been around since the 1600s.

"That's a long time to make enemies," she whispered to herself.

That was about all she had on Priscilla, besides the approximate years she turned Dawn and Isaac into vampires. And she knew next to nothing about Katya, just that she was the oldest there besides Priscilla, since she was the first turn.

Maybe she could shed some light on what was going on since she'd been with Priscilla for so long. But what were the chances that Katya would be willing to share something so personal with her when they barely even talked to begin with?

"Knock knock!" Dawn shouted as she opened Mia's door.

Mia jumped, practically throwing her journal in surprise. She quickly grabbed it and tossed it under her pillow.

"Oh, I'm sorry. Were you in the middle of writing? I can come back later if you're busy."

"N-No, it's fine! Was there something you needed?"

"Oh, well..." she said as she closed the door behind her, and something in her hand crinkled as she did. "I'm technically not supposed to be in here, but I know from experience how hard these lockdowns can be, so I—"

"You know from experience?" Mia interjected.

"I... probably shouldn't have mentioned that." She looked away, ashamed.

"I'm kind of glad you mentioned it, actually. I don't enjoy being in the dark about everything."

"Oh, Mia..." she said sadly.

"So that means this guy has been around before?" She got off her bed and started pacing. "Is he another vampire, too? Why did you have to be locked up? Wait, was it when you were still human?" Mia spat out, not giving Dawn time to answer as the next question popped into her head.

"Mia."

"Why would Priscilla be so afraid of him she'd want to lock you up? Is he—"

"Mia!" Dawn screamed. "Please, stop with the questions!" She looked like she was on the verge of tears. "I'm sorry, but I'm not supposed to talk about it, and I don't want to! Those were not fond memories, so please just... can you not bring them up?"

Mia stared at her. She'd never heard Dawn get so upset before.

"I'm sorry, Dawn. I didn't realize..."

She wiped her tears away and immediately regained her peppy demeanor. "It's fine. Anyway, I brought chips and my favorite comedy movie to cheer you up!" She pulled the bag of chips from behind her back and the DVD from the bag on her waist.

Mia scrunched her face up at the thought of sitting through a dumb comedy movie.

"What's the face for?" Dawn asked.

"A comedy movie? Couldn't you have picked something with, oh, I don't know, a plot?"

"Oh, don't be such a critic. You've probably never even seen this one!" she said, popping the movie in the DVD player and turning on the TV. "Now come on, get over here!"

Mia begrudgingly headed over to the sofa. Dawn pressed play on the movie, and it wasn't long before Mia was out cold from boredom.

CHAPTER THIRTY-ONE

IT HAD BEEN THREE days since Mia's confinement to her room had started, and Dawn hadn't visited her since that first night. Priscilla must be enforcing the rules strictly if Dawn wouldn't even come to say hello to her, not even through the door.

Mia lay on the sofa, tossing a balled-up piece of paper up and down to amuse herself when she heard voices from out in the hallway. She quickly got up and pressed her ear to the door to hear what they were saying. Normally she wasn't the type to snoop like this, but she was getting restless being locked up and sick of all the secrets.

"That means he is getting closer to finding us," Priscilla said nervously.

"Awful bold of him to just leave that body there for everyone to see," Katya said.

"He's clearly trying to send a message," Isaac said.

"Arrogant prick." Katya scoffed.

"Arrogant or not, I cannot allow him to do something like this without consequences," Priscilla said.

Mia heard footsteps and the creak of the stairs.

"Wait, where are you going?" Isaac said frantically.

"He is my responsibility, and I have to do something about it," Priscilla said.

"At least let us come with you!" Katya pleaded. "I know him better than you do. He's malicious, but I might be able to get to him if you just…"

Her voice trailed off as they made their way downstairs.

Mia chewed her nails, the gears spinning away in her head about what this could mean.

If he was Priscilla's responsibility, then that meant she must have been the one to change him, right? But then why hadn't she heard anything about him before?

The front door suddenly slammed, causing her to jump up off the floor. They must have left in pursuit of the mysterious man.

She ran over to the bedside table and grabbed her journal, scribbling down the information she just heard.

There was a huge gap in time from when Katya was turned until Dawn was found… nearly two hundred years. Dawn also mentioned she had to be locked up when she was still human to be safe from this same person, which meant he came around every so often, just like an unwanted family member.

"He has to be one of the family," Mia whispered to herself. "There's no other explanation."

She shut her notebook and hid it away again. If they had all left to go after him, surely it was safe to leave the room?

She walked over to the door, her hand hovering tentatively over the handle. It felt like she was making a terrible decision by leaving, but she just couldn't stay locked in here anymore. She didn't hear Dawn in that conversation, so she had to be in the house still. She had the answers Mia was looking for, and she was going to get them.

Taking a deep breath, she placed her hand on the doorknob and opened it, stepping out into the hallway. The house was eerily quiet again, and it sent a shiver up Mia's spine.

She walked down the hallway to Dawn's door and knocked softly, hoping she was actually in there.

"Dawn?" Mia whispered.

The door opened quickly, catching Mia off guard.

"Mia? What are you doing? You know you're not supposed to be out of your room!" Dawn scolded her.

"I know, but I heard the others leave and I just thought—"

"You thought you'd escape to see me again because you missed me so much? Aw, Mia, you are too kind!" she said, pulling her into a hug. "I missed you too."

"No, Dawn, that's not it," Mia choked out, struggling to get out of the hug.

"You didn't miss me?" Dawn said sadly as she let Mia go.

"I mean, it was lonely without you around… but that's not why I'm here!"

Dawn cocked her head to the side, looking at her, confused.

"I heard Priscilla, Katya, and Isaac talking earlier, and they mentioned the guy I'm supposed to be hiding from and—"

"Mia… I said I didn't want to talk about him…" Dawn stepped back into her room and placed her hand on the door.

"I know, but please, Dawn, I need to know. Is he your brother? Like, did Priscilla turn him into a vampire?"

Dawn sighed, and Mia knew she was right.

"Okay, I'll tell you about him, but just… we have to go back to your room, okay?"

"Deal!" Mia said excitedly, taking Dawn by the hand and leading her back into her room.

Dawn closed the door behind her, and they sat down on the sofa. Mia looked at her expectantly as she pulled out her phone and started typing something.

"What are you doing?" Mia asked.

"Ordering a pizza. You must be hungry, right?"

"I guess, but what does that matter right now?"

"I figure you deserve a little treat with everything that's going on right now." She giggled.

"Okay, but what about this other vampire?"

She clicked her phone off and put it in her pocket. Turning to face Mia, her expression was more serious than she'd ever shown.

"So, you figured out he's my brother?"

Mia nodded enthusiastically.

"Well, his name is William. He was the second person Priscilla ever turned. I guess she found him out wandering the streets in the cold and he was hurt pretty badly? I never cared to ask about the details, but my guess was that his parents were abusive or something."

"So she took pity on him and took him in?"

"That's pretty much how Priscilla works. She can't help but save lost souls like us."

"So then what happened? Why don't you guys ever mention him?"

Dawn bit her lip nervously.

"Because he's a monster," she whispered, keeping her eyes on the floor. "Katya told me she knew from the moment he opened his eyes that there was something wrong with him. He looked crazed, and he went after the deer Priscilla brought him like a wild animal would."

"What do you mean, he went after it like a wild animal?"

"He tore it to shreds. Normally you would just drink a little from it and be fine, but he tore it limb from limb after draining it completely of blood. Almost like feeding from it wasn't enough. He got a high from the kill."

Mia swallowed the bile that rose in her throat at the image Dawn painted in her head.

"It wasn't long after he was turned that he went after his family. He murdered all of them in cold blood, even his little sister, who couldn't have been older than three. Kat said they found him when he was still mauling his father and dragged him away."

"Oh, my god," Mia whispered in awe.

"Yeah, because of that, they were forced to flee before anyone found out what they were and who had done such a thing."

"They took him with them?"

"Yeah, against Kat's wishes, of course. They shook him after about fifty years or so by fleeing Europe into America."

"But he still finds you guys every few years?"

"Only to tease Priscilla for what she's created. He should be dead for all the times he's almost outed vampires to the world, but he always slips away before anyone can do anything about it."

"So..." Mia swallowed, unsure she wanted to hear the answer to the question she was about to ask. "How long does he normally stick around for?"

"A few weeks maybe, but never more than a month. Priscilla wouldn't deal with him for that long."

Mia let out a sigh. She didn't like the idea of being locked in a single room for weeks, but it was better than months or years.

Dawn's phone chimed, and she looked down at it. Her face changed from somber to smiling in an instant.

"Pizza time!" she said, standing up.

Mia stood up as well and followed her out of the room.

"And where do you think you're going?" Dawn scolded.

"To get us some plates from the kitchen?" Mia asked innocently.

Dawn put her hands on her hips and arched an eyebrow at her.

"Oh, come on, Dawn! It's just to the kitchen and back. Besides, Priscilla, Katya, and Isaac are out going after him. If he was here, they would be too, so it stands to reason that I'm perfectly safe."

Dawn chewed on her lip, thinking.

"Fine." She huffed. "But just to the kitchen and back. No dilly-dallying!"

Mia beamed at her and ran for the stairs, Dawn following closely behind. She parted ways with her in the foyer and made her way quickly through the dining room.

As she entered the kitchen, she immediately noticed how

messy it had gotten in her absence. Dishes were piled up in the sink, and the countertops and stove were covered in grime from preparing meals to bring up to Mia.

"Guess I'll have a lot to do once I'm free again." Mia scoffed.

She made her way to the cabinet of dishes and stood on her toes to grab the plates.

"I see Priscilla has found herself another human pet," a sultry voice purred from across the room.

A chill ran down Mia's spine and she dropped the plates on the ground, shattering them at her feet.

"Shit," she hissed out as she turned around, trying to avoid the broken shards on the ground.

There was a tall, lanky man leaning in the doorway between the kitchen and the back yard. He had messy black hair that hung over his right eye, contrasting with his ghostly pale skin. His eyes were blood red as he stared hungrily at Mia.

The white button up he wore was open into a deep V that showed off a large scar on his chest, no doubt from his days as a human. There was blood scattered all over his skin and clothes.

Mia's blood ran cold, and she was petrified as she stared at him.

"William," she breathed out, barely even audible.

A disturbing smile spread across his face. It was the smile of a killer.

CHAPTER THIRTY-TWO

THERE WAS A MURDER in the next town over, a young girl drained completely of blood.

Elliott's heart nearly leapt out of his chest at hearing that news from Zeke. It took him a moment to remember that he would've felt it if that girl were Mia. He would've felt a piece of him die along with her.

"Why would you tell me something like that?" Elliott yelled at Zeke. "You almost gave me a heart attack!"

"Because it means there's a rogue vampire on the loose, and that's not good for any of us," Zeke said, crossing his arms. "Sorry, I didn't realize you'd automatically assume that it was Mia." He shrugged.

Elliott took a deep breath to calm himself down. He walked over and took a seat next to Zeke on the couch.

"So, what are we gonna do about it?" Elliott asked.

"Lie low, like I usually do. It's a good thing I've got a good stash of blood bags hidden in my room to tide me over."

"You're not gonna try to find out who it is?"

"Hey, it's none of my business what other vampires do with their lives."

"Which brings me back around to... why did you even tell me about this if you don't even care?"

Zeke let out an agitated sigh and leaned in towards him.

"Put the pieces together, man. Vampires took Mia, and now one has shown its face in the next town over. It could be a lead. Find them and you might just find her!"

Elliott's heart started beating faster at the thought. Even if it was a slim possibility the two were connected. He had to try.

"Didn't you already check Ardenville for her?" Lucy said as she ran alongside Elliott through the dark forest.

He had her meet him as the sun was going down so they would have a better chance of sniffing out the vampire.

"Tristan and I checked it when she first disappeared, but it's possible they just moved her back into the area," Elliott said.

"Elliott, don't get your hopes up too high. This could just be another random vampire passing through and showing off."

"I'm keeping a clear head, don't you worry. But even if there's the slightest chance of finding her, I've got to take it."

Lucy groaned and sprinted ahead of him.

"You're like a broken record, Elliott."

"Can't help it if it's true."

They came to the edge of the town, shifting back into human form before taking their clothes out from the bags they had tied around their legs.

"So, where did they say they found the girl?" Lucy asked.

"I believe Zeke said it was the center of town?" Elliott said, pulling out his phone and looking up the news article.

"Center of town? Dang, this guy's just asking for us to be outed to the humans."

"Yeah, says here it was the gazebo in Hawthern Park."

Elliott put his phone in the bag and threw it over his shoulder. He started walking, and Lucy quickly caught up to him.

"Don't the vampires have some sort of law against performative killing?" she asked.

"Zeke said sometimes if it's bad enough, they'll send someone to kill them, but I doubt this one murder is gonna attract a lot of attention."

"Hm, that's too bad."

They continued to walk in silence, Elliott leading the way through the winding streets of the town before coming across the park.

"Oh, there it is!" Lucy shouted, pointing at the gazebo.

There was caution tape up around it and the surrounding area, but the rest of the park seemed open to the public.

Elliott sniffed the air as he got closer to the gazebo.

"All I'm picking up is loads of blood. What about you?" Elliott asked.

"Human blood mostly, and some of the cops from earlier. Any trace of the vampire is probably long gone after all the humans investigating today." Lucy frowned.

"Let's take a walk around town a bit to see if we pick anything up."

She shrugged. "I guess it's better than nothing."

They walked for what seemed like hours without a trace of the vampire. Elliott was growing more and more anxious as the night went on. Maybe this was a waste of his time—maybe it didn't have anything to do with Mia at all.

He opened his mouth to tell Lucy they should go home when she suddenly stopped walking. He ran right into her back, but she didn't falter.

"Wait. Do you smell that?" she said, inhaling the air deeply.

Elliott took a big breath through his nose. He almost didn't notice it, but there was a subtle smell of death and pine in the air.

"Vampires," Elliott whispered.

Lucy nodded. "And more than one, it would seem. Maybe you were right."

"Can you follow the scent?" he asked.

"It'll be hard in this form, but not impossible. If we make it to the woods to shift, definitely."

"All right, lead the way."

They walked for an excruciatingly long time along the outskirts of the town before rounding around and heading back in the direction of the gazebo.

"What, did they go back to the scene of the crime?" Elliott asked.

"Shh, they could still be around here," Lucy whispered.

She tapped her forehead, telling him to communicate by their link only. He nodded, and they crept up towards the park, keeping their eyes open.

Then it hit him. The smell of roses from the perfume of the vampire that took Mia.

"Lucy!" he shouted through his mind as he ran through the park, following their scent. "They're here! The one that took Mia is here!"

He dashed out into the clearing behind the group of three vampires right as Lucy's voice rang through his head.

"Don't engage them. We'll want to follow them to get back to Mia! If they know we're here, they won't lead us to her!"

"Shit," he whispered as all three of them turned around as they caught his scent.

There were two females, a redhead and a blonde, and one brunette male, his hair tied back in a bun out of his face.

"Wolf," the redhead hissed at him.

"Priscilla," the blonde whispered to her, shaking her head.

"Hm?" Priscilla hummed, standing up straight and fixing her blouse. "Damn idiot must have drawn him right to us with this murder."

"What do we do?" the boy said frantically. He was obviously the newest vampire there and had never come across a werewolf before.

"We are not here for a fight," Priscilla said, lifting her hands slowly in the air towards him. It looked like she was trying to calm a wild animal, which just made Elliott even angrier.

"You shouldn't have taken Mia then!" he shouted at them. By the shocked looks on the blonde's and brunette's faces, he knew he was right. They had her.

Priscilla's face remained neutral. "I can assure you, we have no idea what you are talking about. We simply came out here hoping to find the cause of the murder from last night. I do not take kindly to reckless behavior like this that could expose us."

"You should tell your friends to work on their poker faces if you want that story to hold up." He growled.

"But it's true!" the boy shouted. He still looked terrified of Elliott.

"You engaged them?" Lucy's voice suddenly shouted in his head. She had clearly snuck up and was spying on them from somewhere.

"Sorry, just kinda happened," he replied through the link before turning back to the vampires. "I don't care what you were doing here. Just take me to Mia and there won't be any trouble."

"We said we don't know who you're talking about," the blonde said, her Russian accent thick as she took a step forward.

"And I said I don't believe you. Your scent was all over the night she was taken."

"You'd wear perfume too if you realized how much you smelled like wet dog," she said.

Elliott let a growl escape his throat, and Priscilla stepped in front of her.

"We are not here to fight you," Priscilla said again. "So please just let us leave in peace so we can track down whoever did this."

"Not a chance." He growled again.

"Then you leave us no choice," she said.

Suddenly, all three of them took off in different directions.

"Go after the boy!" he shouted to Lucy through the link. He seemed the most likely to talk if they caught him.

Elliott bolted after the blonde just as he saw Lucy take off out of a bush after the boy. The vampires were a lot faster than Lucy and Elliott were on foot. If only they could shift, but they couldn't risk that kind of exposure.

The blonde suddenly jumped to the top of the nearest building, and he almost lost sight of her. He caught her scent again and chased her towards the town line. She made the mistake of running into the forest. As soon as he hit the tree line, he jumped, shifting immediately into his wolf form.

He caught up to her easily after that. Pouncing at her from the side, he caught her off guard, and they tumbled through the dirt. He landed on top of her and pinned her arms out with his paws.

He growled and put his muzzle up to her face, baring his teeth. He wanted her to know that he was about to kill her for what she'd done. She shut her eyes and tried to hide her fear, but Elliott could smell it on her. If she wasn't going to take him to Mia, she was going to die for kidnapping her.

He opened his jaw and leaned forward when suddenly a sharp pain ran through his neck. Whimpering, he rolled over as white blotches danced in his vision. He shifted back to his human form just in time to see the blonde girl take the opportunity to escape. He gasped, desperately trying to get air to his lungs when panic set in at what was actually happening.

CHAPTER THIRTY-THREE

MIA'S EYES DARTED BETWEEN the door to the dining room and then back to William. He hadn't moved yet and seemed to be gauging what she was about to do next. She knew he was too fast for her to run out of here; she needed a weapon to protect herself until Dawn came back, but the knife block was all the way on the other side of the kitchen.

The only way she could get to it would be to distract him.

She made a run for the door, and as expected, he beat her there.

"Aw, no, you don't have to run from me, pet," he purred, stepping towards her.

She slowly backed away from him until she hit the kitchen island. She clutched the necklace Elliott gave her for courage.

"I must say, I'm surprised to hear Priscilla told you about me," he said nonchalantly. "I am her greatest shame, after all." He chuckled, a sickening sound to Mia's ears.

"Sh-she didn't," Mia stuttered.

"Oh?" He fake-pouted. "What a shame. I thought she had finally forgiven me."

He seemed to enjoy talking about himself. That was good. It would make it easier to distract him.

She slid along the countertop, attempting to get away from him and towards the knives.

"So, if she didn't tell you about me, how do you know my name?" he said, following slowly after her.

"Dawn—"

"Little Dawny, the tattletale!" he shouted dramatically. "She never could keep her mouth shut. How quiet you are in comparison." He leaned in towards her and sniffed the air around her. "And you don't smell as sweet as she did, but that's a good thing." He leaned in close and whispered in her ear, "I despise sweet things."

She ducked under his arm and continued to move closer to the knife block on the countertop. He smiled mischievously, clearly toying with her.

"This is quite a little dance we've got going here," he commented as he moved alongside her again.

"I..." She gulped, leaning back away from him towards the counter, gripping her necklace again for strength. "I wouldn't really call it a dance."

"No? Then what would you call it?" he teased.

"Not sure, but definitely not a dance." Her heartbeat hammered in her chest.

He turned around and walked away from her, waving his hands dramatically in the air as he spoke, "Oh, pet, if you're going to play this game of teasing me, you should at least come up with some better dialogue."

It was the perfect opportunity to grab a knife out of the block. She quickly swiped a steak knife. She didn't need to kill him, just slow him down until Dawn got back.

"But you know what?" he said, spinning back around to face her as she hid the knife behind her back. "I've been told multiple times I shouldn't play with my food."

Suddenly he was chest to chest with her, and she let out a gasp. He took her chin in his hand and lifted her head up so her eyes met his. They were even more frightening up close, and Mia's heart felt like it was going to pound right out of her chest.

"The drumming of your heartbeat makes this even more exciting, you know," he said, leaning in towards her cheek. His lips barely brushed her skin as he whispered, "I'm going to kill you now."

Her heart beat faster than she thought possible in terror as his lips grazed her throat.

He sunk his fangs into her neck, and a shudder ran through her. It hurt, but it was pleasant at the same time. A feeling of euphoria ran through her for a second, and she almost let go of the knife.

She quickly regained her senses and lifted her arm up before plunging the knife as hard as she could into his shoulder blade. He gasped in pain, releasing her from his hold, and she made a dash for the dining room door.

She was still bleeding from her throat and attempted to put pressure on the wound as she ran.

"Oh, little mouse, you should not have done that!" William shouted as Mia made her way through the dining room, adrenaline pumping through her.

"Dawn!" she shouted at the top of her lungs.

She pushed open the doors to the foyer, blood smearing everywhere she touched. She ran towards the front door.

"Daw—" she attempted to scream again, but the sound got caught in her throat.

Dawn came running through the front door and stopped dead in her tracks. Dropping the pizza box on the ground, a horrified scream ripped out of her.

Mia choked on her own blood as she looked down to realize the knife she had stabbed William with was now sticking out of her throat.

She dropped to the ground gagging, and Dawn ran over to her.

"Mia!" she screamed, before turning to William. "What did you do?"

He let out a bone-chilling laugh. "It doesn't satisfy me to kill her this way, but she had to be punished for stabbing me first."

Dawn bit her arm and stuck the bloody wound into Mia's mouth.

"Drink, Mia!" she begged.

"What are you doing? Her throat has a knife in it. How could she possibly drink your blood?" William laughed.

She didn't answer him, biting into her other arm and forcing as much as she could down Mia's throat. Mia wasn't sure whether she was swallowing her own blood or Dawn's, but she could hardly focus anymore. All she could hear was William's demonic laughter ringing in her ears.

"Come on, Mia, you can survive this, just fight!" Dawn shouted.

"You're gonna wanna pull that knife out so the wound doesn't close around it," William teased.

"Do you think I'm an idiot? That'll just make her bleed out faster!"

Mia heard a struggle behind her and could blearily make out Dawn fighting to keep William away from her, but he was a lot stronger than she was and knocked her to the side.

He walked over and crouched beside Mia with a manic look plastered on his face. He was enjoying all of this.

"Let's hope you actually ingested some of her blood," he said, lifting her back and forcefully gripping the knife handle. "This'll either be goodbye for good or welcome to the family. Kind of a thrilling game of roulette, don't you think?"

He smiled widely and ripped the knife out of the back of her throat. It hurt a thousand times more than when he stabbed her the first time, and she started choking again. She could feel the blood leaving her body quickly as everything around her faded.

Dawn had gotten up and pushed William to the side, shoving

her cut open arm into Mia's throat again, desperately trying to save her.

Everything around her was slowing down, and she became cold. So very cold. The world collapsed into complete darkness. The last thing Mia heard were the sounds of Dawn's cries and William's maniacal laughter as her heart stopped beating and the world went black.

ACKNOWLEDGMENTS

THERE ARE SO MANY people who I would like to thank for making this book possible. First, I would like to thank my friend, Andrea for reigniting my love for reading by lending me so many books from her own enormous personal library. Without you helping me along the way and giving me feedback from the very first draft of Mismet Souls I don't think this book would be where it is today.

I'd like to thank my amazing family for supporting me throughout this journey, and asking about it every time you talked to me, even if I wasn't so forthcoming with the details. The questions kept me motivated to keep going, and to prove that I could actually achieve something like this!

To my awesome coworkers at my day job that would constantly tease me with "how's the book coming?" every time you saw me, thank you for pushing me to have an update for you every day. You guys really helped me to speed up the process of getting this book out into the world, I couldn't ask for better coworkers than you.

I would also like to thank my wonderful editor, Sara for truly making my book as professional as possible. Your encouraging words got me through the editing process and made me more confident as a writer. And my marvelous cover designer and formatter Rena, you made my book come to life in a way I never imaged. Your work is absolutely beautiful, and I am so happy to have had the chance to work with you.

Lastly, I would like to thank you, dear reader, for taking the time to immerse yourself in the world I have created. Without you, none of this would be possible.